Praise for Pornography for the End of the World

"With apocalyptic urgency, Vidito strip-mines our psychosexual fears and frailties as humans to elicit an ecstatic response. I couldn't stop reading. As a grand manipulator, he molds speculative horror and body horror into one dark hybrid, a sleek and cum-soaked vessel of transcendence."

— Joe Koch, *The Wingspan of Severed Hands*, *Convulsive*

"Audacious and devastatingly unique, *Pornography for the End of the World* is the literary equivalent of a Molotov cocktail with author Brendan Vidito's fiery and explosive writing that feels utterly dangerous to read. I'm still recovering from the brutality of some of these tales."

— Eric LaRocca, *Things Have Gotten Worse Since We Last Spoke*

PORNOGRAPHY FOR THE END OF THE WORLD

BRENDAN VIDITO

Copyright © 2022 by Brendan Vidito, Artists, Weirdpunk Books

First Edition

WP-0016

Print ISBN

Cover art by Wieslaw Walkuski

Cover Design by Ira Rat

Editing and internal layout/formatting by Sam Richard

Weirdpunk Books logos by Ira Rat

All rights reserved.

This is a work of fiction. Names, characters, businesses, places, events, locales, and incidents are either products of the author's imagination or used in a fictitious manner. Any resemblance to actual persons, living or dead, or actual events is purely coincidental.

No part of this book may be reproduced in any form or by any electronic or mechanical means, including information storage and retrieval systems, without written permission from the author, except for the use of brief quotations in a book review.

Weirdpunk Books

www.weirdpunkbooks.com

*For Sam Richard, Josie Muller, Charles Austin Muir, Mark Zirbel, and
Lucas Mangum
I can never thank you enough for your friendship...and the binkies*

Contents

WALKING IN ASH

I

"IT'S SIMPLE," DALE SAID, CLUTCHING THE SHOTGUN AGAINST HER chest. "All you need to do is pull the trigger."

The house shook as a bomb exploded less than a block away. The sound was like thunder multiplied a hundredfold. Dale staggered and nearly fell. Her scream was lost in the cacophony of breaking glass and crashing furniture.

Aaron, her partner of six years, stumbled forward and grabbed her shoulders. His eyes were wild, his skin paled by exhaustion and lack of food.

"I know," he said. "But I want you to do it."

Dale shook her head. A solitary tear cut through the grime on her cheeks.

Aaron dropped to his knees like a praying man, hands caressing her outer thighs.

"Please," he whispered.

A second blast rattled the foundations. Dust drifted down the ceiling in a fine snow. The radio perched on the washing machine danced to the edge and plummeted to the floor. Black plastic sprayed in all directions and the batteries rolled across the cement like discarded bones. For months, that radio had fed them news of the world's collapse, but in the last few days, it had offered nothing but the steady hiss of static.

Slowly, reluctantly, Dale lowered the shotgun until the muzzle pointed at Aaron's upturned face. Her finger, with its long, dirty nail, trembled on the trigger. Despite this, she managed to hold the weapon steadily. The skills she gleaned from a lifetime of hunting with her father compressed, diamond-hard, into that singular moment. The window at her back framed an abstract view of hell: red-devil light, obsidian hail, and a ghostly curtain of ash. From his low angle, all Aaron could see of his partner was the towering darkness of her silhouette.

"Quickly," he said. Then: "I love you."

Dale's reply was drowned out by a third, cataclysmic explosion. The force knocked her off balance and she discharged the shotgun. Its roar rose up to meet the music of the world's ending —another jarring note in that symphony of absurd, conclusive violence.

Aaron's head snapped back and his vision filled with red mist. His body hit the floor, legs and arms kicking spasmodically. His bladder and bowels voided in a rush. The blood ebbing from his shattered skull felt first warm, then cold. And on the heels of that observation he realized he was still alive—or at least conscious enough to experience, in some rudimentary fashion, the death throes of his nervous system. He couldn't move, could barely *feel* anything, but was aware of a sensation of loss, as though he had forgotten something vital. Then the answer came to him: three-quarters of his skull had been obliterated. All that remained was one bloodshot eye, his mouth and the shredded remnants of an ear. Summoning his will, he bent his concentration toward his remaining eye and managed to roll it in Dale's direction.

She was holding the shotgun under her chin. Her mouth opened and closed in a series of grimaces. Tears gushed from her eyes. Then, with a wordless scream she pulled the trigger. Gore showered toward the ceiling in a vibrant, glistening fan. The weapon clattered to the cement, followed shortly by Dale's decapitated body, its movements limp and unnatural in the absence of life. She dropped first to her knees, and then flattened on her stomach. The blood from the ragged stump of her neck streamed thickly toward the floor drain.

The fourth explosion leveled the house completely. Brick turned to dust, walls ignited like paper, paint peeled and melted. Everything that had once given the place life or personality ceased to matter in a flash of apocalyptic light.

II

Aaron and Dale had been living in their first home together for a little over a week when they decided to explore the neighborhood. Standing on their front porch in jeans and short sleeves, they quietly took in their surroundings. The sun was setting, its amber glow reflected in the pools of rainwater on the street and sidewalk. Even though it was midsummer, the air was cool, with that clean, rejuvenated feeling that follows a storm. All was quiet like the world had just exhaled, pausing for a moment before its next breath.

Thinking Dale wouldn't notice, Aaron pulled out his cellphone and swiped through the news feed. In recent months, it had become something of a reflex. Each headline screamed a fresh atrocity: two men arrested for plotting an act of right-wing terrorism, a mass shooting at a nightclub that claimed the lives fifty-seven, climate reports warning of worsening natural disasters, and, if the others weren't enough, just that morning various countries had been sparring with threats of nuclear warfare. All it took was a glance and Aaron was instantly overwhelmed. He didn't understand why his mind kept insisting to check the news. It wasn't morbid curiosity. At least he didn't think so. Perhaps part of him thought that knowing what was going on in the world would help dispel the fear. But lately he was becoming increasingly aware that it was having the opposite effect. Every time he looked at the headlines, no matter how cursory his perusal, it was like a solid jolt straight into his amygdala.

"What are you doing?" Dale said. "Put your phone away."

"Sorry," Aaron mumbled, and slipped it back into his pocket.

"You got to stop doing that. We're going for a walk, for god sake."

Aaron laughed nervously and followed Dale down the porch steps.

The couple began their exploration by rounding a corner that led to a part of the street not visible from their porch. It was like they'd stepped into a different part of the city altogether. One ravaged by time and neglect. The street was cramped, hemmed in by dilapidated houses, and the sidewalk rose and fell in jagged rifts where tree roots had slithered up and cracked the concrete.

Aaron and Dale had been aware the area was in the process of gentrification. Seniors and young families populated their street. But what they didn't realize was the gentrification literally stopped dead several doors down from their place. The transition was slightly disorienting, and Aaron's pace faltered for just a moment. He looked back, saw the familiar curve of his street, the blue-painted house that faced his own, and only then did equilibrium return to his mind.

Dale took his hand, threading their fingers together. Her palm was warm and clammy. She cared little for public displays of affection, which suited Aaron fine, but occasionally a glimmer of tenderness shined through, and she couldn't help but express her feelings.

Aaron looked down at their joined hands, then up at her face. She was smiling. The sun glanced off the lenses of her glasses. Her hair was a reddish frazzle, and the slug-thick scar on her forehead—the souvenir of a dog attack in her youth—was highlighted in the dying embers of the day.

Aaron remembered the first time he saw that scar. It was the second time they hung out. She wore bangs then, and shoulder-length hair. They'd gone to the beach with mutual friends on a day when air conditioners struggled to combat the record-breaking heat. Dale had plugged her nose and gone underwater. When she surfaced, her hair was slicked back, plastered against her skull. The scar was bright pink and glistening in the hot summer glare. It was gorgeous. Like jewelry made flesh, complementing the natural beauty of her face. When she noticed Aaron's gaze linger a little too long, she quickly flattened her bangs over her forehead as though covering her naked body. It had taken her several months of listening to reassurances and encouraging words from Aaron before she decided to wear her imperfection with pride.

Now, Aaron asked, "What's up?"

"Nothing," she said. "Just happy. Aren't you?"

"Of course." He gave her hand a squeeze. "I have to admit, though, being homeowners is a little weird."

"Oh, I know," she said. "It beats living in an apartment, though."

"You got that right."

Dale cast her eyes around the street. "It's really quiet here, isn't it?"

They passed a house with a sun-bleached FOR SALE sign and a basketball net in the driveway. Further, on the corner of the street, stood a building of brown brick. It was low and squat. The side facing them was arrayed with three battered doors, each with a number crookedly affixed to the chipped, curling paint. One of them was partway open—the lower half of the gap choked with dirty children's toys and bloated garbage bags. They didn't see any of the occupants. As he looked around for them, Aaron almost tripped over a broken flat screen television lying in the middle of the sidewalk.

"Goddamnit," he said, skipping to recover his footing.

"You okay?" Dale said, barely suppressing her laughter. "Funny how neither us saw that thing until it was too late."

"Daydreaming, obviously. We're not even here a month and we're already turning into mindless suburbanites."

Aaron bent to examine the television. It had been destroyed with chunks of blacktop. Each fragment rested in a crater of smashed glass.

"Someone took out their frustrations on this thing," he said and cast one look back at the brick building before Dale took his hand and tugged him along.

As they turned the corner, Aaron was visited by a sense of déjà vu, accompanied almost immediately by a prickling of dread. It nearly froze him midstride, but he kept walking, hoping the movement would help him puzzle out the meaning behind these sensations. The closest parallel in his mind was the sudden shock of being stung by an insect. Only instead of pain, there was this feeling—just out of reach—that something bad was going to happen.

Ever since he was a teenager, Aaron had been prone to anxiety and panic attacks. And they'd only gotten worse in recent weeks. For this, he blamed both the stress of the move and the endless barrage of fear mongering in the headlines. What he was feeling now seemed very much like the prelude to one of his panic attacks. And if he didn't get things under control soon, his symptoms would only worsen. First, his heart would begin to race. Then came the tingling in his hands and fingertips, followed soon after by unpleasant warmth filling his chest and bringing a flush to his skin. Aaron closed his eyes and took a deep breath. Everything is okay, he mentally whispered to himself. You're taking a walk, and everything is fine. But the dread lingered.

The street they now followed was deeply shadowed, every lawn ornamented by a maple tree with leaves so green it was as though they gave off their own phosphorescence. The road and sidewalks were in much better condition than on their street, and the air was lighter somewhat. Despite the welcome ambiance of the place, however, Aaron couldn't help but sense that it concealed some kind of menace. Horrible things happened here, he thought, hidden away in the shadows. And all the darkened, shuttered windows were blind and ignorant. He shook the impression from his mind. His anxiety was distorting the world around him.

"You okay?" Dale asked.

"Yeah, I'm fine. I'm just getting weird vibes from this place."

"Why? It's beautiful. It looks like something out of a movie."

"Forget it. You know me."

"That you're paranoid?"

She gave his hand a squeeze to show she was teasing. This somehow made him feel a little better.

The tree-shadowed street crested into a hill that branched in two directions. One led to a neighboring street, the other curved down a gravel road. Aaron and Dale halted to consider their route. Silence stretched between them. The symptoms of a panic attack continued to gnaw at Aaron, so he decided to speak up, hoping his voice, once injected into the silence, would reassert his sense of reality.

"I say we continue down the street," he said.

"Aren't you curious what's down there?" she said, gesturing enthusiastically at the gravel road.

"Not really," Aaron answered. "Are we even allowed down there?"

Dale gave him a look that said *don't be ridiculous*. She waved a demonstrative arm. "I don't see a no-trespassing sign."

Releasing his hand, she started down the gravel road, walking backwards, beckoning him with outthrust hands, the fingers dancing in and out of her palms. Aaron stood immobile, watching her with a forced smile canting the corner of his mouth. It was impossible to appreciate her vivacity while his mind continued to simmer with that unknown species of dread. He wanted nothing more than to return home, curl up on the couch and knock back a beer. With any luck, the alcohol would dispel his negative feelings and allow him to slip into a deep, dreamless sleep.

"C'mon, loser," Dale said, vanishing where the path veered around the corner.

"Shit," Aaron said.

He pivoted to look behind him. The street was empty. He turned back to face the path. Cursed again. He had no choice but to follow Dale. Sighing, he started after her. Gravel crunched underfoot. To his right stood a garage without a door. Its depths were smothered in shadow and water dripped rhythmically from the ceiling. Further down the path, a rusted motor home sat in a stretch of yellow grass. Its windows were shuttered with grey curtains of some drab jute-like material. One of them near the back moved subtly as though someone has just retreated from the window. Aaron stared, feeling watched. Something about the curtains didn't seem right. Their movement was unnatural. Before he could make sense of the observation, however, a hand grasped his shoulder, interrupting his line of thought. He gasped, swore under his breath and turned. Dale jumped back, mirroring Aaron's surprise.

"Jesus," she said. "What's wrong with you? Why are you so jumpy?"

Aaron gave another nervous laugh. Looking at Dale, he was quick to realize that her presence no longer offered comfort. His dread persisted, grower stronger with each new intake of breath. He shivered as sweat travelled down the canal of his spine.

"I don't know," Aaron said. "I think we should go home."

Dale's expression softened into concern. Her gaze became more intent.

"Are you not feeling well?"

"I'm definitely not feeling good."

"Are you having another panic attack?"

"I think so."

"What triggered it?"

Aaron paused to consider the question. "I don't know," he said finally.

Dale frowned. "Okay. Let's get going then."

As they turned to retrace their steps, Aaron noticed a house —taller than the others he'd observed in the neighborhood until now—standing at what he assumed to be the end of the gravel path. It was clad in white siding, stained and broken in places to reveal the rotting wood underneath. Graffiti scarred its surface. And through the chaos of tags and vulgarities one message screamed for his attention: I WILL MEET YOU AT THE END OF THE WORLD.

Aaron's eyes then lifted to the only window visible from his vantage point. It was long and narrow. A sickly yellow light burned behind its glass. He could just make out a shadow moving on the ceiling. It was shapeless and seemed to dance with an almost flame-like motion. Aaron blinked, keeping his eyes shut for several seconds. The yellow light remained imprinted on the back of his eyelids. With a flash of pain, it rushed through his skull like a jolt of electricity. Yellow turned to orange, then...*red-devil light, obsidian hail, and a ghostly curtain of ash.* What was that? A memory. A hallucination. His stomach sank. Whatever it was, that brief glimpse of hell and the sickness it carried was inside him now.

III

Some hours later, they were in bed. Faces scrubbed for sleep. Reading lamps glowing in the dusk of evening. Aaron faced the wall, his back to Dale. His eyes were glued to an irregularity in the plaster. It looked like a raindrop on a window, frozen in time. At any moment, it could become a crack that would widen enough to split the house down the middle.

He felt sick. His dread from earlier had mutated into a full-body affliction. He was uncomfortable in his own flesh. His sweat, which came thick and steady from his pores, tasted and smelled different: more acrid and pungent. Acid burned the lining of his stomach. His bones ached, feeling too large for their scant covering of muscle and skin. He wanted to vomit until he escaped this prison of sickness and agony.

The bed springs creaked as Dale placed her book on the bedside table and rolled to face him. Her hand on his shoulder was colder that he remembered. Its chill seeped into his marrow.

"Still not feeling well?" she asked.

"Not quite," Aaron said, still facing the wall.

"Describe it to me."

Aaron thought for a moment, and then said, "It's like a shadow is hanging over my head. And at any moment it could fall and smother me. This probably sounds weird, but I think it's always been there. Ever since—"

He stopped himself, swallowed.

"Ever since what?"

The thought came to him unbidden: *Ever since I met you, ever since we moved into this house*, but he said nothing.

"Never mind." Silence stretched between them. Then he said, "I don't even know what I'm talking about. I'm sure I'll be okay in the morning."

"Well, if you need anything, wake me up, okay?"

Aaron rolled over to face Dale. "I'll be fine. You need your sleep."

She kissed him, gently, their lips grazing as she rolled over again to extinguish her lamp. Aaron did the same. The click of the switch was loud in the relative silence of the house. The only other sound was the quiet drone of the air conditioner. It took a moment for Aaron's eyes to adjust to the dark. Before that, all he could see was black shot with the afterglow of the reading lamp —a pale yellow light that flared red whenever he blinked. He moved into a more comfortable position on his back and waited for sleep. Not a minute passed when he realized it wasn't coming. His mind was fully and horribly awake.

Staring at the ceiling, he listened to music of the air conditioner. It sounded like something alive, breathing loud, icy breath. It had only been a week since they moved into the house, so his mental image of its rooms and layout was imprecise at best. But even so, he attempted to visualize the basement in his mind's eye. It was an exercise his therapist had taught him to calm his mind. *Open the door and you see a washer and dryer, edges flaked with rust. In the middle of the floor, a drain softly gurgles as it swallows the rain fed through the weeping tile. Opposite the laundry machines, stands the furnace, the newest and most polished appliance in that unfinished space. And then, there's the window—small and narrow, looking out from an extreme low angle at the street outside.* It made him think of red light and something else—something poised on the tip of his recollection.

As he explored the space in his imagination, Aaron wondered why he was so engrossed with the basement. It held some form of significance, but couldn't decipher what that was. But he knew it had something to do with that infernal red light. Where had he seen it before?

Feeling movement beside him, Aaron turned and saw Dale watching him through the darkness.

"What are you doing?" he asked.

Her voice sounded drunk and far away, a sleepwalker's drawl. "When I was a kid, my friends and I used to play a game at sleepovers called Wolf," she said. "You'd stare at one another in the dark and watch as the shadows transformed your faces. It gave us a real thrill."

Aaron asked, "Are you asleep?"

"Just play with me," she said. "It's fun."

"I think you're dreaming."

"It'll just take a second."

Feeling like he had no other choice, Aaron stared into Dale's face, tracing its familiar outline and detail with his eyes. For some moments, nothing happened. Her face remained whole, undisturbed by the darkness encroaching from all sides. Then, she began to change.

"Ugh," she said. "You look really creepy."

Aaron didn't know what his partner was seeing. But he doubted it was as horrific as the illusion—it wasn't real, it couldn't be—playing out before his eyes. All the life drained from her features, her eyes rolled back, glazed, the pupils rimmed with ruptured veins. Her tongue hung over her bottom lip, its surface jeweled with droplets of blood. For an instant, Aaron thought he could hear the gentle patter of liquid striking the mattress. It was blood, and it was draining with alarming speed from the missing top half of Dale's skull. An image of the floor drain in the basement flashed subliminally through his mind's eye. He tried to look away, to scream, but he was paralyzed. A quiet moaning began in the depths of Dale's throat, a prolonged death rattle that grew in volume until it engulfed the night silence. Aaron tried again to look away, to cover his ears, to wake up, but it was impossible. He did manage to blink, however, and hellish red light filled his head.

AARON WOKE on the living room floor. It was still dark and the drapes hadn't been drawn over the window, offering him a view of the street. He clambered to a standing position and staggered toward the window. Pressing his hands firmly against the pane, he stared out at the street. It was empty and bathed in the warm glow of the streetlamps. For the first time that night, peace settled on him. He breathed slowly and deeply, wondering why he had ever felt so anxious in the first place. Dale was right. He was unduly paranoid.

But this was a dream. Aaron knew it with a lucid certainty. And so what? It offered him peace he was unable to find at present in the waking world. He would enjoy it. Allow his mind to be swept away on the current of his own subconscious. It would probably do him some—

All the windows across the street exploded with red light. The lamps sputtered and went out. A siren wailed briefly in the distance before falling silent, its echo fading like the filament of a light bulb. Aaron gasped as something slammed into the window with such force it rattled in its frame. Multiple faces stared back at him, charred black flesh stretched in silent screams. Fingers, incinerated to the bone, clawed at the glass with a screeching sound that made Aaron's blood turn to ice. And behind these ghosts of men, women and children, some still burning or smoldering, a white light slowly engulfed the horizon. Aaron threw an arm over his face to shield his vision. But the light was too strong. It penetrated flesh, muscle and bone, singing the vital spark at the core of his being. His scream transformed into the roar of a shotgun blast.

IV

He woke in a clammy sweat. Early afternoon light streamed through the bedroom window. His disorientation was so complete that for several moments he could remember nothing of the past twenty-four hours. Even his dream was nothing but a vague impression. No images lingered or stood out. All he knew was that he experienced something unpleasant, traumatic even, though he couldn't be sure of the details. Maybe that was for the best.

He grunted into a sitting position and glanced at his cellphone on the bedside table. There was a message from Dale. It read: *I silenced your alarm. You were having nightmares. Get some rest. Love you.* He smiled and climbed out of bed.

His dread from the night before had largely dissipated. Only a pale suggestion remained, like a memory on the fringe of consciousness. Today was a new day, and for the first time since the move, Aaron had the house to himself. Dale was going to dinner with friends that night and would likely not return until after he was asleep. It was the perfect opportunity for Aaron to familiarize himself with his environment and get some much-need rest.

He brewed a pot of coffee and lazed around the house for several hours: watching television, reading a book, and eating random scraps of food from the fridge and cupboards. Eventually, his aimless wanderings carried him to the basement, where they had deposited most of their unpacked boxes. They stood along the walls, dour infantry watching over an unpopulated space. He looked at the furnace, hulking and lifeless in the corner of the room. Then his attention fell on a box orphaned from the rest. It sat resting against the wooden support beam in the center of the basement. Dale had written RANDOM SHIT across the top flap in permanent marker.

Aaron walked over and folded the box open. Dale had labeled it appropriately; it was indeed filled with miscellaneous junk. At a glance, he discerned empty picture frames, old, musty books, a loose sock, and a pack of playing cards. He pushed some of the junk aside, and froze as his hand passed over a portable radio that was at least thirty years old. Despite some wear on the corners, it still looked in good condition. And for some reason, it was familiar to Aaron, though he couldn't remember where he'd seen it before. It had likely belonged to Dale's father, something he packed into a box when she first moved out of her parent's place to attend college.

Picking it up, Aaron walked over to the washing machine,

feeling on some deep intuitive level that it belonged there, and set the radio down. The effect was almost immediate. It was like puzzle pieces clicking together in his mind. Though what the puzzle amounted to, he couldn't be sure. He'd merely joined one piece to another. Its full image was still hidden from him.

He glanced at the window. Beyond, the street curved into the ungentrified part of the neighborhood. Another piece clicked together. He swallowed. A new wave of dread welled up from his stomach. What was going on? He had the nagging sensation that he'd caught a glimpse of something vital, and infinitely terrible. But no matter how hard he tried to make sense of it, it was like trying to read a language he didn't understand. He wanted to scream in frustration.

"Goddamnit it," he said aloud.

He desperately needed to put this puzzle together, but what was missing? His gaze returned to the radio on the washing machine. Like a man possessed, he scoured another unpacked box and fished out a pair of batteries. Jamming them inside the radio, he switched it on and adjusted the dial until a human voice garbled into existence. It was a woman. He'd caught her midsentence, talking about the mounting tensions worldwide. Apparently, several countries were in discussions to sign a treaty preventing the use of nuclear weapons in the event of a global conflict. Aaron jabbed the power button. The woman cut to silence.

The basement was still and dark. Quiet except for the steady patter of dripping water. Aaron leaned against the washing machine to support his weight. The dread was creeping back to its original potency, filling his limbs with lead. The hairs on the nape of his neck stood up. What was wrong with him? His anxiety had been a constant presence in his life, but it had never been this bad. Was he in the grip of psychosis? Maybe the stress of the move, coupled with the endless barrage of bad news, had triggered something in his brain.

Somewhere, water continued to drip in a predictable rhythm. He cast his gaze around the room, searching for its source. The ceiling appeared dry and there were no puddles on the floor. Maybe a pipe was leaking behind the wall. He moved around, listening intently. The sound was loudest near the drain in the floor. Aaron hunkered down and lifted the metal grate. A wave of damp air caressed his face. The updraft caused a spider web covering the opening like a membrane to shudder and billow. The web's occupant was almost the size of a quarter. It skittered away and disappeared into the murky depths of the floor drain. Aaron placed his ear over the web and listened. The dripping was undeniably coming from somewhere below. There was nothing abnormal about that. The drain was connected to the weeping tile and it had rained quite a bit the day before. But even with this rationalization, Aaron wasn't satisfied.

He moved the spider web aside, shaking the clinging filaments from his fingertips. Pulling his cellphone from his pocket, he shined its flashlight into the drain. At first, it appeared dry, but when he moved his hand into the square opening, guiding the light deeper, a flash of crimson caught his attention. Rust? Dirty water, maybe? Upon closer inspection, though, he realized it was neither of these things. Reaching inside with his free hand, he touched the crimson substance and rubbed it between forefinger and thumb. It was sticky and oddly warm. Aaron reached in again with the intention of acquiring a larger sample. With an animal shriek, the red substance darted deeper into the drain. Aaron flinched back with a cry of his own, and crawled across the floor to the opposite side of the room.

His back was to the washing machine. His chest rose and fell, and his breath emerged in ragged, panicked gasps. Thunder pulsed inside his chest with every frantic beat of his heart. Then the sobs came, each one threatening to wrench his lungs up his throat. He was losing his mind, there was no longer any doubt about that. The notion terrified him. He couldn't imagine a worse reality than not being able to trust one's own mind. He couldn't be alone any longer. He needed Dale. To hear her voice, feel the touch of her hands, smell the fragrance of her hair. She would make things right again.

He dialed her number. She picked up on the second ring.

"Getting bored having the place to yourself?"

Aaron tried to speak, but choked on a sob.

"Aaron? What's wrong?"

"Can you please come home?" he said. "I think something's wrong with me."

"What happened? Are you hurt?"

"No." He shook his head. "The feeling from last night. It's getting worse."

There was a pause on the other end of the line. Aaron could almost hear her mind working. Then she said, "Okay. I'm on my way now."

"Wait."

"What is it?"

He took a deep breath before speaking. "Do you think it's possible to be haunted by something that hasn't happened yet? Something so horrible, it vibrates backward through time?"

"Aaron, what are you talking about?"

"The signs are all there. In the news. On the radio. I think something terrible is going to happen. And I'm the only one who knows it."

The more he spoke, the more his words seemed right. More puzzle pieces fitting together to form a progressively clearer image. It hovered in his mind's eye, bleak and imposing. A tableau depicting him and Dale collapsed on the basement floor, bathed in blood and ash.

"Listen to me," Dale said calmly. "Nothing bad is going to happen. Just hang tight and I'll be home as soon as I can. Okay?"

"Okay," he said, though it was barely audible.

He hung up and leaned his head back against the washing machine. Dale's office was only a fifteen-minute drive from home. It wouldn't be long before he heard her voice calling him from the living room. He closed his eyes and waited. A trickle of sweat ran down his forehead. His heart continued to beat a frantic tattoo against his ribs. Everything was going to be okay, he mentally told himself. Dale would make everything better. For as long as he knew her, she had a way of making the world seem like a less frightening place. All he had to do now was wait.

V

He opened his eyes. Night had fallen. Darkness lay thickly over the basement and its disorder of unpacked boxes. Aaron gasped and shot to his feet. It had only been two in the afternoon when he closed his eyes. He checked his phone. A little past one in the morning.

"What the fuck?" he said, his voice shaking.

He checked his call history. Nothing from Dale. He dialed her number and waited. It rang and rang, and just as he was beginning to lose hope, she answered.

"Where are you?" Her voice sounded far away, distorted by static.

"Downstairs."

"Come up," she said.

He moved toward the staircase. There were no lights on upstairs. And everything was quiet. Something wasn't right. He mounted the first step. It creaked loudly under his weight. The second step sounded a note of its own, equally jarring in the ringing silence.

His phone vibrated in his hand. He held it at arm's length, checking the display. A text message from Dale read: *It's simple...* Then the phone buzzed again and a second message appeared: *All you have to do is pull the trigger.*

"Dale?" he called upstairs.

No answer.

Once on the main level he turned to face the hallway leading into the bedroom. Dale stood at the end, unmoving, little more than a dark shape. *All Aaron could see of his partner was the towering darkness of her silhouette.* He flinched at the mental image that sprang into his mind and superimposed itself on the scene before him. He took a step toward Dale and stopped. Something held him back. All of this was familiar, but it wasn't until Dale held up her hand and spoke that he realized he was living a scene from one his nightmares.

"Do you want to play Wolf?" she asked.

The world outside exploded with red light that streamed

through every window and doorway. It washed Dale in a visceral glow. She smiled and her teeth gleamed as though washed with blood. Her hair, Aaron realized, was styled the way it'd been when he'd hung out with her at the beach those many years ago—bangs swept over her forehead in a concealing curtain. Now, she raised her arm higher, and using an index finger parted the hair to one side, exposing her scar.

For several seconds, Aaron's mind refused to process what he was seeing. When it finally started working again, he shuddered in horror. He tried to scream. To run. But he was paralyzed. Rooted to the spot. He could only watch helplessly as Dale's scar opened like a mouth and expanded until it split her face down the middle. There was a loud crack as her skull came apart and a mixture of blood and brains fountained upward, splashing against the ceiling in defiance of gravity. Her eyes, each one nested in a separate half of her face, stared wildly, shining with perverse enthusiasm. Her tongue, like the rest of her head, had been ripped apart. Two bloody chunks of flesh waggled like bloated worms inside her mouth.

Another nightmare, Aaron thought almost casually. His fear upon seeing Dale, as it turned out, was short lived. It loosened its grip on his forebrain and faded away. In its place, came sadness—a feeling of profound, inexplicable loss. For the span of a moment, he was a child again, curled in bed, and reeling at a world didn't yet understand.

Dale walked toward him. Gore continued to waterfall from her skull, leaving a clotted red river on the ceiling behind her. She took his hand, threading their fingers together. Her palm was cold, the fingers stiff and clumsy. Aaron found that he could now move. He turned to look at Dale, and in spite of himself, managed a brief, sad smile. Even now, she had a way of making the world seem like a less frightening place. He would always love her for that.

"I don't want us to die," he said.

"So, you understand now?"

"I'm not sure. All I have is this feeling."

"You will never fully understand," Dale said, her voice lisped. "That's the mercy of premonition."

"Will this feeling ever go away?"

"Everything you've experienced these last few hours began on our walk," Dale said, as she conducted him toward the entrance. "Let's take another and see what happens."

She opened the door. It was dark outside. A crimson glow throbbed on the horizon. Flakes of ash fell like snow, and a trumpeting hum filled the air.

They moved onto the porch and stared at the street. Swarms of adults and children fled for their lives. Some were still on fire, others had been badly burned, their skin hanging from the bone and smeared in the fluid of broken blisters and liquefied fat. They were hairless, and their eyes had melted down the sides of their faces. Only their teeth were undamaged, bared in soundless screams of agony. None of them appeared to notice the couple on the porch.

Still holding Aaron's hand, Dale led him down the steps, across the driveway, to the sidewalk. They started walking in silence, following the same trajectory from the evening before. When they reached the bend in the road, Aaron experienced comfort rather than disorientation. He felt like he'd taken this walk many times before. Its geography and landmarks were familiar to his memory. Some distant, lucid part of his mind told him he should be driven mad from the vision of horror all around him. But, instead, he found himself nursing a dull, manageable fear.

"Watch your step," Dale said.

Aaron looked down. A broken flat screen television lay in the middle of the sidewalk. Its power cable snaked through the grass, useless and limp. Despite being unplugged, however, the screen flashed brightly and a garbled half-human voice emerged from the speakers. Through a dense web of cracks and dead pixels, a face was either laughing or screaming. The couple didn't stop to observe it more closely. They kept walking, soon rounding another corner.

Here was the street deeply shadowed by trees, only now their leaves had been burned away. All that remained were the trunks and branches, alternately blackened and bleached by the force of some unknowable catastrophe. As a result, their shadows had grown thin, like emaciated fingers reaching across the asphalt for mercy or supplication. Behind every window lurked a face, screaming and charred black. In one home, a mother and father were killing their children with steak knives to spare them of further suffering. The youngest took the blade to the chest with innocent willingness, while the eldest had to be caught and pinned to the floor, allowing the father to cut his throat like a sacrificed lamb.

Aaron wept for them, but again continued walking. Dale wouldn't let him stop. She instead guided him up a gravel road. When they reached the motor home at its end, she stopped and said, "I leave you here. You must continue on your own."

He turned to face her and cupped her bloodstained cheek.

"I don't want to lose you," he said.

"There is nothing to lose when we all die together," she replied.

Aaron could barely comprehend the elation he experienced upon hearing these words. They served as a climax of sorts—the much-needed respite after a long journey. Up until now, his entire existence had been consumed by anxiety. He'd been walking in the ashes of things to come. But now, Dale had blessed him with peace of mind using only a mouthful of simple words. He inhaled and the air shuddered into his lungs.

"Why am I seeing this?"

"An accident," she said. "You weren't chosen, if that's what you're wondering. The universe is blind. It doesn't choose anyone for any specific purpose. You merely contracted something on your walk the other night. A splinter in your a brain, a flash of things to come."

The trailer shuddered on its cinder blocks. Aaron looked over Dale's shoulder and saw the curtain rustle and fall away with a muffled thump. A sliding, shuffling sound travelled the length of the vehicle, before the door burst open and something slithered into the grass. It was grey and thin, like a massive flatworm, and its flesh had the texture of old jute. What Aaron had originally mistaken for a curtain was, in reality, something alive. It moved through the grass with a whispering sigh, raised the upper portion of its body from the ground and regarded him intently. Aaron had the sudden impression of invisible fingers reaching into his mind, beckoning him forward.

He spared one final glance at Dale before following its sinuous course toward the house with the graffiti. Soon the words: I WILL SEE YOU AT THE END OF THE WORLD loomed above him. He looked up at the only window visible on this side of the building. Light and shadow wrestled in a wild orgy, twisting and turning like elongated limbs wracked by spasms. Something was moving in the upper room.

The flatworm-thing stopped at a door that hung ajar. Sickly yellow light spilled from between the gap. Aaron looked at the creature. It was motionless. He turned his attention back to the door, took a step forward, and wrapped his fingers around the handle. With a deep breath, he swung it open. Light painted his face and stunned his vision. He held up a shielding arm. When his eyes adjusted, he found himself at the foot of a staircase. Feeling like he was on the verge of waking from a long nightmare, he gripped the bannister and started to climb.

It didn't take him long to reach the top. The room was modest, no more than a storage space. The yellow light seemed to emanate from the air itself, as though the particles of dust that drifted about were endowed with a form of bioluminescence. The shadows he perceived from outside had appeared on the ceiling. When he looked up, the blood vessels in Aaron's eyes engorged with blood and exploded, rendering him blind. His head swam and he nearly lost his balance. Either his eardrums ruptured or his brain was so overloaded with what he'd just seen on the ceiling that he could hear no more. Despite being both deaf and blind, however, Aaron still possessed a vivid picture of the ceiling dweller in his mind's eye.

It was vaguely humanoid, though at least three times the size of the largest man. It was curled up in the fetal position, its massive head cradled close to its knees. Long white hair hung down from its mottled scalp, each strand moving of its own accord, casting erratic shadows across the walls and floor. Its eyes, much too large for its face, roved madly in their sockets.

Aaron staggered backward until his spine came into contact with the wall. As he stood there, his mind a firestorm of questions, fear and confusion, the thing on the ceiling began to speak. Its voice rumbled in his bones and rearranged the cells in his body. It told him, in a language without words, that the human race would soon come to an end. The humanoid-thing, along with his kind, would inherit the ashes once the world had grown silent and barren.

The force of its speech drove Aaron to the floor. Blood pumped warmly from his ears and spilled down the sides of his face. He opened his mouth and screamed, "Why me?" over and over in a demented refrain until the pain in his head grew to engulf his entire being.

VI

He woke the following morning in bed, to find Dale snoring softly beside him. For several minutes, he didn't move. His eyes were fixed on the ceiling. Had Dale also been awake, all she would have seen was a white surface dappled with sunlight. Aaron, however, saw much more. His vision had expanded overnight. A huge man, not unlike the one Aaron had encountered in his dream the previous night, was curled up on the ceiling. Perhaps he had always been there, watching. Aaron stared at the man-thing, and it stared right back with bulging, bloodshot eyes. Its mouth moved in slow motion. It was speaking, and though Aaron couldn't discern the words, he understood their meaning. It was counting down.

Aaron climbed out of bed and moved into the kitchen. The man-thing followed, sliding along the ceiling with its arms pinned to its sides. Aaron gave him little heed as he turned on the coffee machine and threw a piece of toast in the toaster. He then turned on the radio, making sure the volume was not loud enough to wake Dale. He ate his meal and drank his coffee as the newscaster droned on and on. Eventually, Aaron realized she kept repeating the same story in an urgent loop, informing potential new listener of what they had been missing. He stopped chewing, put down his coffee.

War.

He closed his eyes and thought of the day he spent at the beach with Dale. Every image, every impression flitted across his mind. The heat of the sun. Trees painting the shore a rich emerald green. Seagulls wheeling and crying under an unbroken blue sky. Dale's face sheened with lake water. The first time she *really* looked at him, appraising him as a future lover and friend.

God, he loved her.

He opened his eyes again, stared at the remains of his breakfast. Above him, the man-thing continued to count down. Aaron was ready for what waited at the end of those numbers. His dread and anxiety was nothing but a memory. There was no reason to be afraid anymore.

A floorboard creaked behind him. Turning, he saw Dale, standing in the hallway. Her hair was disheveled, her eyes puffy with sleep.

"What's going on?" she asked.

MOTHER'S MARK

IN THE MIDDLE OF THE NIGHT, THE FISSURE ON HER APARTMENT wall bulged and disgorged a man encased in an amniotic sheath. He struck the decaying floorboards with a pulpy crack, white fluid pooling around his huddled form. The woman crouching in the corner of the room—impatient for this moment—stood up and approached him. The sensory organs on her face danced in response to this new and intriguing stimulus. Already, she could feel herself growing wet with desire. Hopefully her latest experiment would yield positive results.

Rolling up the sleeves of her satin robe, she used one fingernail to slice an opening in the amniotic sac. Clear liquid gushed out, washing over the ruptured sheath and diluting the white substance already spread across the floor. The woman reached inside. Nutrient sacs and capillaries tangled in her fingers as she probed for the man's forearm, gripped it, and pulled. The Mother's Mark, wrapped like a living tattoo around her upper arm and shoulder, glowed a faint orange in the gloom. Its blessing coursed through her muscle fibers, imbuing her with the strength necessary to lift the man to his feet and hold him in a clumsy standing position. His legs were unsteady, their musculature hardening and springing into shape as she watched.

He was a handsome specimen, two fingers above six feet and broad in the shoulders. His body and head were devoid of hair or follicles. His mouth was lipless and filled with long, narrow teeth designed for sexual biting. The woman had also outfitted his skull with biological accessories intended to enhance pleasure: lubricating orifices, an organic vibrating module, and pores that excreted a sensation heightening gel. The woman held his shoulders, looked up into his face. He certainly looked better than her previous efforts, but the true test lay in his functionality and abilities.

She glanced around the room to ensure she was alone. It was cluttered with broken and dirty laboratory equipment. The apartment's electricity was being funneled into a massive chest freezer that hummed like something alive. Inside were the pieces of organic matter she indented to recycle from failed experiments—she had eaten the rest, roasting the flesh over a propane stove. The four corners of the bachelor were occupied by birthing nodules the woman had recovered from the street, where they had fallen from the sky bound body of the Great Mother. They had long since metastasized into the building itself, allowing her experiments to transition from wet dream to reality.

Her senses honed on the single blacked-out window. Beyond was the city with its rivers of flesh and the Great Mother watching from above. As always, the woman would have to ensure her experiments remained a secret. The Great Mother had eradicated the male species for a reason, and any attempt to reconstruct or resurrect their kind was punishable by death.

She passed a hand over the man's face, her sensory organs droning a reverse lullaby. The man shuddered violently, breath surging into his body. Mere seconds elapsed as he acclimated to his environment, and then he was upon her, grasping her waist with sinewy hands, and pressing his mouth against her neck. The woman moaned softly, curling her fingers around his biceps, and tilting her head back to encourage his advances. His teeth pinched her flesh and pulled, sending a white-hot streak of pain through her nerve-endings. A little too hard, she noted, but that could easily be adjusted. Then he spun her around, tearing the robe away in a flash of gleaming crimson, and squeezed her breasts. Hot, pheromone-laced breath panted against her neck. His cock, eight inches long and studded with fat deposits to increase pleasure, rubbed against the cleft of her ass. She tried to loosen his grip on her, but he only tightened his hold so she could barely move. Memories of past, failed experiments flooded her mind. Not again, she thought. Why couldn't she breed the primal aggression from her subjects? Was it so firmly rooted in their sexual identities? Not for the first time, the woman wondered if this violence was the reason the Great Mother had purged them from existence.

The Mother's Mark flared a bright orange. The woman effortlessly pulled herself away from the man. Spun around. Gripped the sides of his head. And decapitated him with a casual upward motion of her hands. Blood pumped from the ragged hole in his neck, and his body collapsed, twitching, to the floor. She tossed the head into a corner of her room and looked down. A thick stream of seminal fluid trailed away from his softening erection. The woman hummed disappointment. Another failure, but at least she would have something to eat tonight.

Apate's Children

Glass shattered and something heavy thumped on the living room floor. Caiden shot up from his sleeping position on the couch and scanned the darkness for any sign of a threat. First he noticed the hole in the window. Then his gaze travelled to the floor, where he found the source of the destruction, a rock roughly the size of his fist. He got up too quickly, and the blood rushed to his head. Swaying, he bent down, picked up the rock and turned it over. The rough, grey surface was stained with two bloody handprints—child's handprints.

Not again, Caiden silently pleaded. *Not so soon.*

His fingers convulsed. He drew in a sharp breath and dropped the rock. Wet blood shimmered on the ball of his thumb. He rubbed it frantically on his pajama bottoms and backed away until he collapsed on the couch. Fear laced with guilt burned through his veins. The children—those sadistic, ruthless little pricks—had returned. He would be needed tonight.

Focusing on his breathing, he slowly got up again. He worked his way to the kitchen table, opened his laptop and selected the security system icon on his desktop. The house he shared with Susan was situated in a bad neighborhood— burglaries, assaults, and vandalism were regular occurrences. A combination of necessity and paranoia had compelled Caiden to invest in home security. However, in recent months, the system had been used to monitor a threat unlike anything he could have anticipated.

The laptop screen was divided into six windows, each corresponding to a separate area of the house: the front porch, the back door, the hallway, the garage/driveway, the back yard, and the kitchen. All cameras were switched to night vision mode, turning once familiar environments into monotonies of light and shadow. Caiden scanned through each window. Nothing out of the ordinary. He leaned closer. And jumped. There was a flash of movement near the garage. His first thought was a raccoon looking for food. But the memory of the rock and its bloody handprint prevented the possibility from fully taking shape in his mind. Seconds later, as though to confirm his error, one of the children stepped in view of the camera.

He wore a stained, threadbare sweater with a hood, the sleeves hanging limp below his hands. His face was only partly visible, smooth and pointed with eyes that glowed in the ghost light of the night vision lens. He shot quick darting glances around the driveway before staring directly into the camera. Caiden frowned, swallowing the dry, sickly sweet taste in his throat. The child seemed to hold his gaze for a moment longer, and Caiden's body reacted as though he were in the presence of a predator—which in a way he was. Cold sweat broke over ridges of gooseflesh. His jaw tightened to a hard, painful line. Adrenaline sang through him like clashing cymbals. He blinked, and when he focused on the driveway camera again, the child was gone.

Caiden shook his head and laughed bitterly. He knew what was coming. It had been occurring with greater and greater frequency over the last two months. As always, his will resisted, every fiber staining against the inevitable, but in the end, his inner struggle concluded with a flat note of resignation. He deserved everything that would be visited upon him tonight.

A cascade of memories flooded through his mind. Susan's round smiling face. Snapshots of trips they had taken together. Her low, chuckling laughter. All the things she had done for him.

And you betrayed her, said an internal voice that sounded uncannily like his own.

His shame conducted him down the hallway. Cracking the bedroom door, Caiden was greeted by a familiar drift of warm air, scented faintly by Susan's slumbering breath. From the thin trickle of light bleeding through the doorway, Susan was visible as a hump under the bed sheets, the ebony spill of her hair like a shadow on the pillow. Caiden focused his gaze on her motionless form for a moment longer, not wanting to turn his attention to the shape he knew crouched at the foot of the mattress. It had been there every night since—*her skin fever hot and scented faintly of sweat...the soft fullness of her ass in his hands...the taste of liquor and nicotine on her tongue...the racing, uneven rhythm of his heart... the growing sickness and shame roiling inside him*—since what happened, happened.

Swallowing dryly, he finally broke his gaze from Susan. As usual, the visitor—the architect of his penance—crouched at the end of the bed, amorphous and yet distinctly feminine. Its stomach, vast and distended, seemed to encompass the room. Shadows pulsed and radiated from the central mass of its body, transforming the walls and ceiling into an extended womb. Its hands, attached to thin, stick-like arms were wrapped with maternal tenderness around Susan's waist and the back of her head. One finger languidly stroked the thin hair on her temple. And throughout these ministrations, Susan remained motionless, wrapped in careless slumber.

The guilt that festered inside Caiden metastasized, rampaging through him like some necrotic infection. His knees grew weak, his head filled with static, and nausea roiled in the pit of his stomach. He staggered away from the bedroom, pulling the door shut as he went. The assault abated, but only slightly. As he walked into the kitchen, he continued to wrestle against the nauseous pangs that threated to rise into his throat.

Pulling open the junk drawer—where they kept everything from sandwich bags to packing tape—he rooted around until he found a crumpled pack of cigarettes. He went outside through the side door and lit up. The cigarette was stale, the dry, bitter taste clinging to the roof of his mouth. He smoked anyway, spitting occasionally into the grass to make the experience more palatable. Glancing at the street, through the gap between the neighbor's house and his own, he noticed the lamp on the corner was extinguished. The road was dark, the houses on the opposite side nothing more than rudimentary shapes and hazy textures.

As his cigarette neared its filter, Caiden's attention was drawn to the dining room window next door. The ochre wall, adorned with a sentimental work of needlepoint, was splashed with a vertical red stripe. It confused his sense of recognition, like finding a familiar location in a dream subtlety altered. That crimson stripe had not been there earlier. He and Susan passed that window multiple times every day, registering its existence either directly or peripherally. It was visible not only from the side door, but the kitchen window, and constantly appeared to watch them as they prepared dinner, like a great jaundiced eye. No—that red scar was new, an anomaly, a blasphemy against the comfortable normality of his everyday existence. His stomach turned over. He knew what was coming. There was no stopping it now.

Mashing his cigarette against the house, Caiden jumped the fence into his neighbor's yard and strode to the front door. It was open slightly. Light from within bled through a two-inch crack. Caiden knocked, called out. Nothing. He heaved a sigh, recognizing the silence as its own unique form of answer. He had been summoned. Now he was being led, as in a dream, to the meeting grounds. He opened the door and stepped inside.

A body lay stretched on the kitchen floor, its lower extremities visible from the entrance. Caiden approached with slow, measured strides. It was face down, clad only in jeans. Dark, almost maroon blood pooled around its midsection, shimmering under the ceiling fixture. An infantile figure straddled its hips. It rose from the corpse like a trapdoor on a rusty hinge. The skin on the lower two-thirds of its face had been peeled back to reveal the stained and blackened bones of its jaw. The jaw bones were packed tight with clusters of adult teeth. They trembled slightly as the child moved. In one tiny, blood-slick hand it held what could only be a fragment of rib bone sharpened to a dagger point. This assumption was confirmed when Caiden noticed the gaping wound in the child's side. The edges were oleaginous with blood, the organs and remaining rib bones on full display.

The child raised the rib bone and plunged it into the back of the corpses' neck. Blood squelched and oozed lazily down. Pushing its hand into the puncture wound, the child pulled out a cluster of veins and sinew. It shone wetly, strands of bright white standing out among threads of brown and crimson. To Caiden it looked absurdly like an inverted bouquet of roses.

The hand squeezed, releasing a gush of blood diluted with lymphatic fluid. It was a gesture both demonstrative and accusatory—*look what I have to do because you will not give me what I need.* Caiden was disgusted how quickly he interpreted the child's pantomime. It was as intuitive as a silent exchange between lovers. He shook his head. His foot dragged across the floor as he took a step backward.

"I can't," he said, his voice ragged with emotion. "It's too soon. You only just—"

The child released the cluster of flesh—it slapped wetly against the corpse's neck—and stood up. Its movements were jerky, abrupt—stop motion in fast-forward. Opening its flayed jaw, it clacked its teeth together, the din ringing through the silent room.

"I can't," Caiden said again, though now the words were robbed of conviction.

It was true. He had little sustenance to spare. The children had fed only two nights ago. Nevertheless, he had no other choice. Such was the nature of his punishment. Caiden forced down his fight-or-flight instinct and closed the gap between him and the child. It looked up with empty sockets and opened its mouth. Caiden focused on the yawning blackness of its throat. His vision irised to a dim spot of light, then blinked out altogether.

CONSCIOUSNESS RETURNED in a surge of nausea and terror. *Not here. Not again.* The words echoed hollowly in Caiden's skull. He opened his eyes, knowing what he would see—and yes, here he was again, that hellish landscape he had come to know as the Extraction Chamber. It looked like his bedroom, but the ceiling was traded for a sky dense with cloud. A diffused light from some star or moon illuminated the floor, which was carpeted with dozens of naked bodies, their flesh packed so tightly no trace of the laminate was visible.

Each had a face Caiden recognized—be it a member of his family, a friend, or colleague—and they regarded him with cold, unblinking disdain. He tried not to return their gaze as he followed the child to the middle of the room, but their eyes possessed a strange gravitational pull, drawing his vision down into their ocular depths.

The extraction table—as Caiden understood it—stood at the center of bedroom, a few feet away from the bed, and consisted of three white marble statues arranged in reclining positions. All were female, with wide hips and thighs, and small, round breasts. Their hair, cut short, caressed the sloping downward curve of their skulls.

As he had done innumerable times before, Caiden removed his clothing and climbed onto the table. The marble was icy against his feverish skin. Within seconds, he began to shiver. His teeth chattered. The child, now joined by a score of its brothers and sisters, reached under the table and produced a thick needle-like device attached to a cable the color of bleached flesh. With its free hand, the child palpated the skin under Caiden's ribs. He flinched at the shock of its cold, hard fingers. Then, without ceremony, the child plunged the pointed tip of the device into Caiden's stomach. The pain was incandescent. No matter how many times he suffered through this experience, it never got any better—and that, he assumed, was the intention. His pain was to be consistent and terrible.

With reluctance, he looked down where his body wedded with the device. At first, the wound gushed a torrent of steaming red fluid, then the pump under the table began to work with a vicious hydraulic hiss, and his blood was replaced by a thick black bile.

Moving his gaze away from the gory mess on his stomach, Caiden followed the fleshy cable across the floor, up to the bed, where the beautiful, but terrible visitor presided over Susan's sleeping form. Using one of her long arms, that dark goddess—for what else could she possibly be—gripped the opposite end of the cable and pushed it between her lips. The bile filled her mouth and leaked down her chin, and even in the low-light Caiden saw her throat rise and fall in a series of voracious swallows. When she was sated, she extracted the cable—it spurted the last dregs of bile over the white sheets—and grinned at Caiden with her immaculate teeth. Despite his agony, Caiden returned the smile, blood trickling down his lower lip.

BEFORE HIS PENANCE, before the black goddess and her skull-faced brood, Caiden and Susan were seated together on the living room couch. Tears flowed warmly down Caiden's cheeks. His confession came in halting bursts. Susan absorbed it in silence, betraying no emotion, watching him with an odd sort of curiosity. It was the first time she had seen him cry.

Please react. Please show me something, Caiden thought, confused and terrified.

And throughout his confession, he sensed a second pair of eyes boring into him from somewhere unseen. Watching. Assessing. Though he could not explain it, he understood the gaze belonged to something hungry, something that stalked him with glassy, blood-crazed eyes.

Finally, Susan opened her mouth. Her eyes had become empty sockets. Her lips peeled back to reveal the blood-soaked bones of her jaw. In a voice that was too harsh to be the woman he had come know and love over the past six years, she said, "*She is the crafty one...eater of men...mother of mothers...punisher of the unfaithful. Apate. Apate. Apate."*

HE WOKE in bed with a start, covered in his own blood. The space beside him was empty. Reaching out, he ran his fingers along the shallow impression Susan had left during the night. With a shuddering breath, he started to get up. The bed sheets clung to his back and arms as he peeled himself from the mattress and set his feet, squelching, on the floor.

Standing now, he touched the place on his stomach where the device had penetrated. The skin was smooth and unmarred, except for a layer of clotting blood. Despite the lack of physical damage, however, the pain still lingered—a dull stabbing sensation that spread down his torso whenever he breathed. There was nothing he could do to alleviate it, weeks of bitter experience had taught him as much. He would have to do his best to ignore the pain until eventually it faded to an unpleasant memory.

He followed the smell of coffee to the kitchen. Susan stood by the sink, washing her favorite mug. Dish soap foamed over the lip and dropped into the basin. She half turned, smiled sheepishly at Caiden, and set the dripping mug on the counter.

"Good morning," she said.

Pulling the hand towel from the oven handle, she dried the mug with slow, careful motions. She was facing Caiden now, clothed in an oversize t-shirt and worn moccasins. Her gaze travelled down his body. Like before, if she noticed the blood, she gave no indication.

"Sleep well?" Caiden asked.

Susan poured her coffee. Steam role in a curling plume.

"Yes, I did. Thank you for asking."

They watched one another in silence for a beat. The blood varnishing Caiden's body dripped monotonously on the floor. Susan frowned, set her mug on the counter, and wrapped Caiden in an embrace. He held her tightly, his face buried in her hair. The curves and hollows of her body felt strange, unfamiliar —though not unpleasantly so. She was both remote and intimately close—a dream on the brink of recollection that could vanish at any moment.

"Everything will be okay," Susan said. "I just need time."

Her breath, and the words it carried, danced across the nape of his neck, sending waves of electricity down his back. Reluctantly, Caiden began to disengage from their embrace, but something across the room diverted his attention. He stared, numb, at the window above the sink. Beyond, the dining room next door beckoned with its bright, ochre wall. The piece of needlepoint mocked him with its normalcy. The red slash from the night before was gone. And as Caiden separated from Susan, he saw an identically shaped smear of blood across her face, from where she rested it on his shoulder. She looked up at him, her expression neutral.

He swallowed, opened his mouth to speak, but no sound emerged. He tried again, gently gripped Susan's shoulders, "Take all the time you need."

From somewhere unseen, glassy, blood-crazed eyes sparked with hunger.

THE HUMAN CLAY

LIAM HEDLAND KNEW THE STREETS LIKE A PALMIST KNOWS THE lines of a hand. His knowledge was especially keen where the more dangerous parts of town were concerned. He was intimately familiar with every shadow and alleyway, every tenement and drug den. And that awareness provided him with the advantage he needed as a trafficker of illicit biological material. Organs, both synthetic and natural. Infectious agents. Potent pheromones. Implants. The biohazard cooler in the back seat of his delivery van always contained one or more of these items, ready for transport to high-paying clientele and underground medical organizations.

It was the only job in a long line of odd jobs that was suited to his disability. He was able to remain seated for extended periods, avoiding the use of his legs—which grew rigid and painful after limited intervals of movement. In a way, the delivery van was part of his treatment. The necessity to remain behind the wheel acted as a form of passive rehabilitation, supplementing his daily dose of painkillers and anti-inflammatory drugs. It was a glorified wheelchair, a steel and leather extension of his damaged body.

Now, as he drove through the streets sheltered in the warm, soft embrace of the painkillers, Liam considered tonight's destination: the home of his boss, the famed geneticist and criminal kingpin, Anton Halverson. Running his fingers over the steering wheel and narrowing his eyes against the glow of the street-lamps, Liam wondered why Anton had called him over at this hour. It was the second time he had been summoned directly to Anton's home, where he lived with his wife and three children. On the previous occasion, he'd been given the most important and dangerous assignment of his career—a delivery that ended with Anton's closest associate, Kane, taking a bullet to the throat.

They'd been less than a block away from the delivery point— Kane riding in the passenger seat with a shotgun on his lap— when a person on a motorcycle pulled up beside them and fired a pistol through the window. The biker wore a helmet with a black, mirrored visor. Doubtless, they were attempting to steal the cooler in the back seat. As far as Liam knew, it contained some form of biological weapon. That was the reason Kane was riding along.

As soon as the bullet pierced the side window, Liam stomped the gas pedal and weaved through traffic as the motorcycle growled in pursuit. Eventually, he managed to escape, using his knowledge of the streets to his advantage. The feat, however, did little to alleviate his sense of failure. His boss had outlined a specific route, and Liam had deviated from it, presuming he knew a more efficient course. In a way, he was responsible for Kane's death.

The incident had troubled Liam greatly. He doubled his dose of painkillers, losing himself in a netherworld of dulled edges and swirling grey mist. Whenever his mind drifted, he remembered the way the glass spider-webbed around the bullet. The groan and wet gurgle that escaped Kane's mouth as the bullet pierced his throat. And, above all else, his own reflection, pale and blood-flecked in the rear-view mirror. He feared punishment from Anton, anticipated it with every knock on the door, every phone call, but it never came.

Waiting at a stoplight, Liam dreaded to think what the eminent geneticist had in mind for tonight's house call. Was his employment with Anton Halvorson about to end? Had his punishment finally arrived? Or was he in store for something totally unexpected?

After several minutes and an endless string of traffic lights, Liam reached the suburban hills overlooking the city. Massive homes flanked immaculate streets and well-lit sidewalks. A few late-night wanderers moved like sleepwalkers through the dusk, walking dogs or heading toward unknown destinations. Watching them as his cab rolled slowly down the street, Liam realized he felt like a stranger to these people—an altogether different species.

When he reflected on his appearance, he didn't see the slight paunch or the atrophied stalks of his legs. Instead, there was the rusted contours of his cab, the worn treads on the wheels, the scratches and finger-smudges on the windows. He liked to think of himself as the brain or beating heart of a much larger, mechanical organism—vital but anonymous. For so long, his body had betrayed him, denied him even the most basic human needs—from sexual inability to occasional bouts of incontinence —that he favored an existence that melded his defective flesh with reliable machinery. It made his biological shortcomings a little more bearable.

The sight of Anton's home pulled Liam out of his reverie. He pulled up along the sidewalk outside the gate. Visible through the gilded, wrought iron bars, was a paved driveway lined with solar-powered lights. At its terminus stood a French Normandy mansion, its windows hemorrhaging a serene yellow glow.

As Liam stared, the gates opened abruptly with a grating sound. At the end of the path, the door to the mansion, nothing more than a black square at this distance, was replaced by that familiar wash of golden light. And within it, framed by its brilliance, was a tall dark shape. The shape moved slowly toward the gate like a figure in a nightmare. Liam watched, as though in a trance as the shadow grew larger, more sharply defined. Then a clunking sound, followed by the chime of the door alarm, made him jump in his seat.

The passenger door opened and Anton slid into the seat. He wore a slimming grey suit that matched the shade of his combed-back hair and trimmed beard. His eyes were pale blue, and he had a kind, thin, effeminate face—enhanced no doubt by plastic surgery—reminiscent of an angel from a Renaissance painting. He clapped a hand on Liam's shoulder and squeezed.

"It's been too long," he said through his teeth. "How've you been?"

His smile was contagious. Despite his apprehension, Liam felt the muscles at the corners of his mouth loosen and rise. "I'm okay," he said, voice flattened by the pain pills. "You know, same shit."

"How're you feeling?"

Liam blinked at him, knowing Anton saw the glossy sheen in his eyes, the pallor of his skin. Anton pursed his lips and nodded, completing the silent exchange. Their relationship ran deeper that superior and employee. They understood and respected one another. Now and again, communication could be achieved through physical expression alone.

Liam shifted into drive, made a U-turn and started down the street. Once he reached the first set of lights he turned to Anton and asked, "Where are we going?"

Anton pointed vaguely at the windshield. "Head toward the borough. Morovian Place, know it?"

"Yeah." Liam dragged the word out slowly, summoning a mental image of the area—rundown commercial buildings, broken asphalt, faded graffiti and reclaiming weeds. A nearly forgotten corner of a decaying, volatile neighborhood. Did anyone live there besides derelicts and habitual drug users? As far as Liam knew, it was practically abandoned, a domain of shadows and starving rats.

A flutter of anxiety pierced the fog of the painkillers. Liam's fingers twitched and drummed the wheel. "What's on Morovian Place?"

Anton tilted his seat back and stretched out his legs. He heaved a sigh that filled the cab with the scent of peppermint. "I realized I never thanked you for your assistance in the whole Kane affair." Liam flinched at the name. "Seeing him die couldn't have been easy. But despite that, you successfully completed the assignment. And, for that, I owe you my thanks."

Liam blinked. Was he hearing him correctly? Was Anton actually thanking him for safely delivering the weapon, even though Kane bled out in the passenger seat? He decided not to question Anton's assessment of the situation. He allowed the news to wash over him.

"Is there a five-star restaurant on Morovian I don't know about?"

Anton barked a short laugh. "Can you imagine?" he said, then shook his head. "No. There's something much better."

The seat complained under his weight as he angled his body to further face Liam. The driver glanced briefly in his direction, saw the light of the city play in a kaleidoscope across his angular face.

"Your condition," Anton said. "I remember you telling me it presents you with limitations. Especially of the sexual variety."

Bitter, embarrassed laughter spilled from Liam's throat.

"You know that?" he said. "How fucked up was I when I told you?"

"That's irrelevant," Anton replied. "As you know, my passion and vocation are human genetics. I see in you a problem I want to fix, or at the very least, address to a point where your life becomes a little more accessible."

Liam frowned, not knowing where this line of reasoning was heading. "What are you implying? What's on Morovian?"

"My brothel," Anton said with a half smile. "A playground of flesh and metal."

THEIR DESTINATION HAD ONCE SERVED as a gynecology clinic. The building was square and dilapidated, its grey brick stained by rivulets of dark crimson where rust had leaked down from the rain gutter. Sagging wooden steps ascended to the front door, which was flanked by wide, blacked-out windows. The place gave the impression of a long-neglected mausoleum, still and silent.

Liam brought the cab around the building to the rear parking lot. A sputtering lamp beside the fire door fitfully illuminated two figures. A man was on his knees, while a woman stood facing him, pointing a gun at his forehead.

"What the hell is going on?" Anton said, watching from the passenger window.

Liam eased on the brake and cranked the gearshift into park. Anton stepped out, long graceful strides carrying him toward the man and the woman. Liam fumbled the keys out of the ignition, clumsily stuffed them into his pocket. He opened the door and paused. Warm wind caressed his face and rustled the dirty napkins stuffed into the cup holder.

A feeling of naked vulnerability overcame him. His heart was a fist, tight in his chest. With a tender motion, he ran his fingers along the fabric of the driver's seat, taking in its aura of comfort and familiarity. Stepping out of the cab always brought with it a vague anxiety. It was like shedding an article of warm clothing and stepping out into treacherous weather. The sensation held Liam in its grip for several moments, as it always did, then he heaved a deep sigh and exited the vehicle.

His legs, too thin for the jeans that enclosed them, wobbled unsteadily on the cracked asphalt. He took a limping step forward, then another, shambling in clumsy pursuit of Anton. As always, Liam was acutely aware of how his knees bent inward, giving his gait the fragile jerkiness of an injured bird. He willed the image from his mind, gritting his teeth in frustration, and labored forward. He instead decided to focus on what was taking place before him.

"Carrie," Anton called out. "Everything under control?"

Carrie darted her foxfire-green eyes in his direction. She had a pointed, elfin face, an upturned nose, and shoulder-length blonde hair. Her charcoal grey work suit was rumpled as though from a struggle, and as he approached, Liam could see—clearly outlined in the glow of the streetlights—the downward curve of her breasts, sheened with perspiration, a hint of eroticism in this tableau of confusion and potential violence.

With her free hand, she languidly pushed several stray locks of hair from her eyes, keeping the gun trained on the man's forehead. He was middle-aged. His lips were pulled away from his gums and his eyes rolled like he was a cow on the path toward slaughter. He was also, Liam now realized, wearing nothing but ill-fitting underwear.

"Everything is fine, Dr. Halverson," Carrie said. Her voice was high, but devoid of inflection. "This gentleman disobeyed the rules of the house. Apparently, my words of warning weren't enough. I had to use other means to entice him out of the building."

Anton stepped up beside Carrie, examined the man before her coldly, and then turned his gaze to the weapon clasped between Carrie's manicured fingers. "Is that what I think it is?"

"Yes," Carrie said.

Anton nodded toward the man. "What do you plan to do with him?"

"He's certainly not coming back here."

Liam joined them, peering between their shoulders at the man. He met Liam's gaze and flung out his hands in a gesture of supplication. "This is a huge misunderstanding. I won't breathe a word about this to anyone. I have no reason—"

The gun in Carrie's hand popped—a hydraulic thud followed by a wet hissing sound. The man's head snapped back. His eyes fluttered. His mouth opened and closed in a series of silent gasps. Instead of a bullet hole, a raised black lump the size of a grape marked his forehead. As Liam watched, dark veins spread out from the lump, twisting under his skin as they stretched across his face like a tar-soaked spider web. Throughout this process, he remained mute and unmoving, his eyes glazed. Then, abruptly, his forehead erupted into balloons of putrid, cancerous flesh. The jagged edges of his shattered skull thrust outward through a corona of bruised and bleeding skin. Tainted lymphatic fluid gushed from the wound in steady streams. Melanomas clouded and cracked his eyeballs with purple, distended veins. With a loud crunch, the tumors in his forehead expanded throughout the remainder of his head. His gums blackened and his teeth oozed from their sockets, tinkling against the asphalt. His tongue expanded, filling the cavity of his mouth. He let out one final, strangled gasp before slumping sideways, his legs twitching feebly.

"Jesus Christ," Liam said. "What did you do to him?"

Carrie said, "I made him malleable."

Without turning her gaze away from the dead man, she lifted the gun demonstratively. It was roughly the same size as a 9mm pistol, though the edges of its barrel were wide and rounded. The metal gleamed like polished steel. It gave off a faint odor of decomposition.

"This is a highly coveted tool. We lost one of our greatest men transporting it some weeks ago." Was she talking about Kane? She had to be. "A single projectile spreads a voracious cancer throughout the body in seconds," Carrie went on. "It also makes the flesh more…expressive. Transforms it into clay that can be kneaded by inspired hands."

She turned to face Liam. Held out her free hand. Liam stared at her fingers for a beat, visualizing them working a lump of wet clay, before finally shaking.

"Why did you kill him?"

Carrie shrugged. "He was dangerous." Her nearly bioluminescent eyes flicked to the collar of her button-up shirt, where the fabric was stretched to reveal the swell of her cleavage. "And he touched me."

Anton placed a hand on each of their shoulders. "Liam, meet Carrie, one of my biotechnicians and the den mother of this establishment."

"Pleasure," Carrie said. "And, Dr. Halvorson, I'm a sculptor, not a biotechnician."

Anton nodded. "Of course." He smiled apologetically. "Shall we go inside?"

Carrie watched each man turn. "Good idea. Dr. Halvorson, bring the body in with you."

THE INTERIOR of the brothel defied Liam's mundane expectations.

A chorus of moans and screams, blended with wet sucking sounds, played over speakers mounted on the walls. The light fixtures on the ceiling were long and conical. They shed a crimson radiance over the space. The marble floor was made up of dizzying swirls of black and white, like a melted chessboard. A grainy hologram shone on the wall opposite the back door. It comprised a disembodied face, huge and Oz-like, with androgynous features and a perversely grinning smile. Liam thought he saw it move: a twitch of the eyeball or crease of the brow, but it could have been his overwrought imagination.

To either side of the hologram, video screens had been mounted to the walls. They showcased close-ups of genitals in act of union; lips pressed against one another, and fingers boring into orifices. All these high-definition loops were intercut with extreme close-ups of worms wriggling in their own slime and maggots feasting on decomposing flesh. As Liam stared transfixed, both types of images became indistinguishable.

When he finally managed to look away, he noticed the mural on the ceiling. The artist had rendered, with a touch of madness no doubt, Adam and Eve's story from Genesis. The first scene depicted Satan—horned, cleft-hooved, and with exaggerated genitals—communing with the first man and woman. The second had them eating the forbidden fruit, which covered their faces and fingers in blood-red nectar. The subsequent tableaux showed Adam and Eve fucking in various positions, culminating in Adam eating the womb out of Eve. A pale, dying Eve participated as well, taking a tentative bite from her reproductive organ.

"Beautiful, isn't it?" Carrie said. "The paint is made entirely from biological material."

With Carrie in the lead, they entered a room the size of a

small banquet hall, dimly lit by red pot lights. The walls were painted black and lined with an array of pedestals and rolling gurneys. On each sat a shape wrapped in shadow. They moved feebly, hinting at some form of life or automation.

Liam scanned the room with trepidation clawing up his spine. The three of them stood in the doorway. Crimson light bathed Anton's face, distorting his divine features into something demonic. He said, "Liam suffers from a wasting disease that has made him unable to participate in sexual activity."

"Anton, come on," Liam cut in, heat rising in his cheeks.

Anton held out a restraining hand.

"It's fine. You're among friends."

"There's nothing to be ashamed or embarrassed about," Carrie said.

She gripped Liam's hand and threaded her long, thin fingers through his.

"Dr. Halverson only wants to help you," she continued, guiding him to the nearest gurney. The pot light overhead flared to greater brilliance, illuminating the thing writhing on its starched sheets. "This place is unique. We can break through your impotence."

It was a woman's torso devoid of head and limbs. The stumps were smooth and pale with scar tissue. Its skin was porcelain, unblemished and inviting to the touch. A light growth of pubic hair framed a delicately sculpted vulva. The torso undulated in an erotic wave, the muscles of its abdomen tensing and releasing in rippling spasms.

"Touch her," Carrie said, gently taking Liam's wrist and guiding his hand toward the thing on the gurney.

He was resistant at first, but as soon as the warmth from the torso's flesh reached his fingertips, he relented. She was incomparably soft. It was like stroking a breath of summer wind. The torso shuddered, gooseflesh spreading over its curves and folds. A thin steam of clear lubricating fluid oozed from its vaginal opening.

"You made this," Liam said. It was less of a question, more an awe-stricken statement.

"She is one piece in a gallery full of my art," Carrie replied, fanning out her arm in a gesture that encompassed the room.

"And people come here to—" Liam started, and then fell silent, a frown creasing his forehead. "I don't know how this place will help me." He glanced at Anton, then back at Carrie. "I haven't been intimate...I haven't been *able* to be intimate since this happened to me." He gestured sharply from his waist down to his old, battered shoes.

Carrie touched him on the shoulder and guided him to the pedestal beside the gurney. The light overhead grew brighter, dousing them in a sanguine glow. It took Liam a moment to process was he was seeing, his brain struggling to draw disparate elements together into a coherent whole, seeking patterns. It appeared to be a mound of intricately layered flesh, an exotic flower of labial and scrotal tissue threaded with filaments of metal. Liam stared, hands dangling at his sides as the thing heaved with a vaguely respiratory movement.

"There's something here for everyone," Carrie said. "I have found a way to abbreviate the human form to a purely sexual organism. These creations possess antibodies strong enough to combat any infection or disease. Their sole purpose is pleasure, free of guilt or worry."

"I still don't understand how that will help me," Liam said.

Anton injected his voice into the conversation. "You need to show him the thing downstairs."

Silence prevailed for a moment. Carrie and Anton exchanged glances, appearing to come to an understanding, and then both focused their attention on Liam again.

"Do you care to see?" Carrie asked.

"I don't know what's going on," Liam said and looked pleadingly at Anton. "Why did you bring me here?"

"To help you," Anton said without hesitation.

Liam shook his head, confused and overwhelmed. Whatever vague expectation he had upon entering the brothel was rapidly evaporating in a mist of anxious uncertainty. Had Anton been telling the truth? Did he truly intend to show Liam a good time as a token of his appreciation, or was something more sinister in the process of unfolding? Whatever the case, Liam knew better than to panic or question his superiors, especially someone with the influence and cold pragmatism of Anton Halverson. And besides, the two were more than employer and employee; they were friends, were they not?

"Don't be alarmed," Anton said, easily deciphering the look on Liam's face. "This is something you want to see."

THE BASEMENT WAS a maze of boxes and defunct office equipment. Carrie pressed a button at the bottom of the staircase and a row of tube lights flickered into existence. Despite the disorder, the room was well kept: the floor swept and polished, every surface unmarked by dust. The air even smelled faintly of disinfectant and pine needles.

Liam passed a hand over the top of one of the many boxes stacked throughout the room. The words "CERBERUS BIOTRONICS" were printed across the side. He assumed it was the name of one Anton's suppliers—a purveyor of black-market pharmaceuticals and biotechnology.

"It's through here," Carrie said, indicating a walled-off portion of the room. A steel door marked "Do Not Enter" stood out against the pallid drywall, which ended halfway to the ceiling. Beyond, orange light painted the walls and a huge, amorphous shadow stirred with movement. Liam strained his ears and caught the sound of breathing, heavy and phlegm soaked.

He took a step back, flicked his gaze toward Anton, who smiled.

"It's one of Carrie's sculptures. There's nothing to fear."

Carrie extended her hand and twisted the handle with agonizing slowness. Liam's pulse pounded in his ears, sweat trickled down his back. The door finally opened, and he nearly choked on the breath he was holding when he saw the thing on the floor sitting in a puddle of semen and excrement.

It had the body of a man, hairless and pot-bellied. Its chest sagged, pendulous breasts hanging halfway to a stitched navel.

Disproportionately large thighs shimmered with a thin coating of seminal fluid. Its lower extremities were a dysfunctional marriage of human feet and cloven hooves. Black keratin burst out from between half-formed toes and split the soles into uneven halves, making anything other than crawling impossible. A corkscrew-shaped organ trailed on the floor between its knees. It was half a foot long and raw from excessive friction.

Its head, however, was the most grotesque feature of all. It didn't belong on the shoulders of a man, but the bloated, humped body of a pig. Glassy, black eyes rolled in their sockets, a sickle of white visible along the edges. With an inquisitive grunt, it raised its snout and scented the air. Mucus trickled from its pulsating nostrils. It took in the three visitors and blinked dumbly, its lips quivering away from disturbingly human teeth.

"What happened to him?" Liam said, his voice unsteady and weak.

"He wanted a deeper communion with his own sexuality. He approached me with a request of enhancement. I've performed such procedures before, but this time I wanted to attempt something unique."

The swine creature lifted its head and unleashed a guttural scream. Liam flinched.

"In extreme cases, a boar is capable of having an orgasm that can last up to thirty minutes. Imagine it, an orgasm that sends you into a prolonged state of euphoria, a sexual high seemingly without end. Once this epiphany struck me, it was only a matter of putting my sculpting skills to use. You see... sapiens and swine aren't very different on a genetic level. The clay of their flesh blends nicely together."

"Why are you showing me this?" Liam asked, though an answer was already forming in his mind. He had assumed correctly when he received the summons from Anton earlier that night. His punishment had finally arrived.

Anton clapped his shoulders and squeezed. "Liam, I respect you deeply. And I want to ensure that your life is complete." The usual placid cast of his face melted into an expression that combined both sadness and regret. "What you allowed to happen to Kane was unforgivable. Had you been anyone else, I would have ended your life the moment the news reached my ears. But you're a close friend. So, I decided you wouldn't be punished. I want nothing but happiness for you. And my expertise has allowed me to give you something your condition has denied."

Liam thought of running, but his legs were too weak to accomplish the task. Instead, he grasped Anton's hand on his shoulder and squeezed, like a lover seeking comfort. The guilt and anxiety that had been roiling inside him for the past few weeks was finally beginning to slough away, replaced by a sense of resignation...of peace.

"I understand," he said, his voice cracking. "I appreciate everything you've done for me."

Anton nodded. "It'll be quick."

A loud pop behind him. Something slammed into his back. There was a sudden pressure, a cold burning sensation. He collapsed into Anton's waiting arms.

"Thank you," Anton said into his ear. He pushed him and he stumbled boneless into the room with the swine creature. Anton and Carrie stood framed in the doorway, the latter holding the tumor gun in a lazy grip. It exuded a faint stench of decay. Liam closed his eyes and dreamed as the cancer invaded his body, turning him to clay.

HE LAY on a plain of raw, bleeding flesh. All around him stood cairns constructed of bone and fragments of rusted metal. The sky was the color of an open wound. Thunder sent shockwaves through the atmosphere. At length, Liam became aware of a wet, shuffling sound. It was steadily growing louder, approaching from every direction. He rolled his head to one side. A swine creature pulled its body across the fleshy landscape, dragging useless legs behind it. Liam scanned the rest of the perimeter and confirmed he was surrounded by a score of such creatures, crawling toward his prone, cancer-ridden body. Grunts and screams filled the air.

"You're a eunuch who dreamed of carnal pleasure," said a voice. "And now, you're awake."

Liam lifted his head. Kane stood at his feet completely naked, his body streaked with crimson. The wound in his neck pumped a steady stream of dark arterial blood.

"I'm so sorry," Liam said.

Kane shook his head. "Leave that all behind you."

The swine creatures were close enough that Liam could feel their breath against his skin. They leaned in as one and sank their teeth into his arms and legs. He closed his eyes expecting agony, but he had lost all awareness of his physical body. Gone were the imperfections, the inequities, and the pain. Everything was warm and weightless, and soon, wave after orgasmic wave crashed into his being, flooding him with an overwhelming rush of never-before-experienced sensation. He screamed, drowning out the tearing and chewing sounds of the swine creatures. His orgasm grew exponentially, swallowing, digesting, and dissolving him into protoplasm of pure, raw euphoria. Finally, his evolution complete, he opened his eyes.

And awoke into a realm of endless pleasure.

THE CHIMERA SESSION

THE WORMS WRITHED IN A BOWL OF OIL AND LEMON JUICE. THEIR bodies were thick, smooth, and dark as raw liver. Each bore a vaguely human-shaped head with slanted, empty eye-sockets and a closed vertical slit that appeared to be a mouth. According to the waiter, they had marinated overnight and were ready to be consumed.

Jillian reached into the bowl and pinched one of the creatures between her thumb and forefinger. It wriggled in her grip, sending flecks of brine into the air, dappling her cheeks and forehead. A single drop hung on her lower lip, noticeably heavy. She tasted—a hint of salt, acid, and something else, an earthy tang she assumed belonged to the worms. Almost immediately, the tip of her tongue went numb. She let saliva collect in her mouth, swallowed, and only then did the sensation fade.

She glanced at Michael, seated across from her at the mahogany table. He smiled, lips pursed, looked down at his hands. His foot tapped restlessly against the floor. What was he thinking? He seemed anxious. Annoyed.

His distraction was contagious, apparently, because she found her gaze drifting away from him. The dining chamber was in the basement of an office building, its entrance accessed by a narrow alley. It was roughly twenty feet across, fifteen feet wide, and lit by a chandelier. Its walls were painted a deep shade of crimson, and music—Mozart's "Lacrimosa"—played quietly on a gramophone in the corner. A nondescript door divided the chamber from the kitchen. Muted voices and the clanging of dishes brought a domestic ambiance to an otherwise surreal and somewhat unsettling atmosphere.

A clock ticked on the wall, though it possessed no hands or numerals. A fish tank in the corner opposite the gramophone hummed softly. Its azure glow bred shadows that entwined the couple like black ivy. Jillian felt her eyes drawn toward its hypnotic light. Behind the glass, fish darted around spires of artificial coral. A juvenile eel emerged from the depths and sinuously made its way toward the surface.

"What's wrong?" Michael's voice shattered her concentration.

She was tempted to roll her eyes at the question. If anyone should be asking what was wrong, it was her. In the previous months, Michael had gone from an enthusiastic and affectionate partner to a relative stranger, monosyllabic and withdrawn. At first, she suspected he was having an affair. The issue, as it turned out, was not so sensational. As they lay in bed one night, they realized their relationship had reached the terminal stage of its existence. Jillian had felt it too, though she was slow to admit the truth.

The question then became: what do we do now? It seemed wasteful to simply discard five years of hard work and co-habitation. In the end, they decided to work on their bond. But after months of taunt tempers, dead-end conversations, and unfulfilled desires, they decided more extreme measures would be necessary. That was when they heard about the Chimera Session.

At the dinner table, Jillian shook her head. "I'm fine," she said. "Are *you* okay? You seem distracted."

Michael shrugged. "It's just—I don't know how this," he gestured expansively around the room, "or this," he stabbed a finger at the bowl in the middle of the table, "will help us."

"It doesn't hurt to try."

"Has it occurred to you we're doing some kind of weird

swinger's retreat?"

"It's much deeper than that," Jillian said. "And besides, we're not swinging if it's just us."

Michael watched the worms undulate in their bath of brine.

"Maybe," he paused for a moment, swallowed. "Maybe, we're over. Maybe it's easier to walk away."

The muscles in Jillian's face sagged. Do you actually want our relationship to end, she thought, or are you simply too unmotivated to make it through the evening? "If that's true, then let's try to enjoy one last experience together, okay?"

That pursed smile again. "Okay."

She extended the worm, still wriggling, across the table toward Michael's face. He recoiled, his chair complaining at the sudden movement, and leaned forward again. His mouth parted and Jillian guided the worm inside. Michael's eyelids snapped closed, and his face distorted into a mask of disgust. He bit down, chewed in abrupt, staccato movements, and swallowed.

"That feels really weird," he said. "My throat is going numb."

"My turn," Jillian said.

Michael reached into the bowl and removed another worm. It thrashed violently. He cupped his other hand under it to catch the dripping brine and guided the creature over the table toward Jillian. She opened her mouth. The worm slithered around, smearing her tongue and hard palate with its anesthetising mucus. Her teeth closed on one end of the worm, and its other half went rigid, pressing against her gums. Another bite, and her tongue was flooded with a vaguely nutty flavour. It wasn't unpleasant. Before the numbness overwhelmed her taste buds, Jillian relished its complexity.

It tasted of fresh almonds, earth, blood, semen, and the salt on sex-drenched flesh. The flavours altered and blended, growing more complex—more indescribable—as the macerated worm travelled down her throat. But her scrutiny was short-lived. With a flash of intuition, Jillian understood the purpose of the anaesthetic agent. It inhibited the taste buds, kept them from appreciating the worm for too long. Human gustatory perception was ill-equipped to understand the majesty of its flavour.

The numbness spread down her throat, filling her chest and weighing down her stomach with warm, pleasant heaviness. A ringing started in her ears, low-pitched at first and steadily growing louder. She slid her gaze down to her hands, which stood out pale and small against the dark surface of the tabletop. As she stared, her skin blurred, losing detail and definition. The flesh loosened and began to run like melting candle wax. The liquefied flesh curled and eddied, pooling around her knuckles, trickling down her fingers. And as the motion continued, the smooth pallor of her skin gave way to other hues and textures: olive, dark brown, callused, baby-smooth, wrinkled.

"Michael, are you seeing this?"

She looked up, eager for his reaction. His chair was empty. The gramophone droned on, noticeably louder. Jillian blinked. No fear touched her, no confusion, or anger. She understood his absence was part of the Chimera Session.

All she had to do now was play her role.

Reaching into her pocket, she pulled out her cellphone and opened the Chimera dating application. The icon depicted the silhouette of a creature with multiple heads: a lion, a ram, and a dragon. She logged into her account with the password provided by the waiter. A notification appeared onscreen.

COLIN WANTS TO MEET YOU FOR DINNER.

The circular image above the message showed a handsome, middle-aged black man. Jillian tapped the message, bringing up a virtual keypad. Her thumbs hovered over the keys for a moment as she considered her reply, then she began to write.

HELLO COLIN. WHAT DO YOU HAVE IN MIND?

Her message appeared as a pink bubble under Colin's invitation. A second notification manifested—a prompt from the application itself.

HELLO MIRANDA. WOULD YOU LIKE TO SHARE A PICTURE?

Jillian smiled. Her lips felt fuller, her cheeks rounder. It was like she was wearing a mask—or a face that belonged to someone else. She acknowledged the prompt and the camera application opened, showing her the new configuration of her face. Rounded cheeks, plump lips, green eyes replacing her brown ones, straight black hair so unlike her curly strawberry-blonde tresses. She moved the camera down her neck, to her chest, revealing heavier breasts and full hips. Tattoos formed along her arms as she watched, snaking across her dark skin, taking the forms of enchanted greenery and mythical creatures —the dermal scrapbook of another life.

Jillian adjusted the phone and the camera pointed at her new face once again. She smiled with unfamiliar lips and teeth and snapped the photo.

The worm had taken effect, and the session had begun.

MIRANDA MET Colin at a Japanese restaurant on the edge of town. The date began with sake and polite conversation. As Colin spoke—his voice deeper and more resonant than Michael's—Miranda watched his lips move, visualizing them grazing the curves of her new flesh. The space between her legs grew warm; her heartbeat throbbed against her eardrums.

Their waitress finally arrived with sushi and sashimi artfully arranged on a porcelain tray. The couple removed chopsticks from cloth sleeves and began to feast. With the chemical influence of the worm surging through her veins, each mouthful doubled as an aphrodisiac. Miranda's body responded to every bite with a shudder. An identical reaction played subtly across Colin's features. A band of sweat glistened along his hairline. He grinned and wet his lips. They shared their meal in silence, feverish anticipation building inside them.

Miranda ceased to recognize herself as Jillian wearing a new skin. Her former identity dissolved in the rapture of the moment, as did most of her memories of Michael. All that remained was the imperative to repair what was broken—mend a bond with someone she loved more than anyone else. And that someone had transcended the individual, becoming an idea, a longing that could now be expressed, without restraint, through the blessing of the Chimera Session.

When they'd finished dinner, the couple shrugged into their coats and moved outside. Rain fell in a steady drizzle, sparkling around the lamplights. Umbrellas bobbed down the sidewalks and cars rolled by, sleek and reflective. Miranda took Colin's hand and guided him into an alley. The brick walls wept, rain spilling from the eavestrough. She pushed him roughly against the wall and slanted her mouth over his, licking between his lips and flicking his tongue. His chest shuddered under her palms. As the rain covered them, Miranda felt like her skin was melting, sloughing away like acrylic escaping its canvas. She opened her eyes, still pressed into Colin. Their skin had lost its smooth appearance, and it moved like a wave, turning their individual pigmentations a greyish-blue. Miranda understood—in what she could only ascertain as dream logic—that she and Colin were undergoing some form of transformation.

A scream pulled them apart. Their bodies twitched back to their human configurations. A woman holding an umbrella stood a few paces away, staring at them. When they turned to look at her, she shrieked again and fled with brisk, splashing strides.

Flushed, breathless, and shaking with laughter, they hurried onto the sidewalk. Colin hailed a cab. They climbed inside. It drove for fifteen minutes in silence—the couple holding hands in the back seat—before it stopped in front of an unfamiliar brownstone in the heart of the city.

Miranda and Colin ducked out into the rain, hurrying up the front steps. Colin produced a key from his jacket pocket and fitted it into the lock. The door opened onto a dark hallway. He slapped the wall, searching for a light switch. A dusty fixture on the ceiling illuminated narrow stairs flanked by brownish red walls. They ascended and reached a hallway shared by three apartments. Colin opened his hand and examined the key resting in the center of his palm. Peering over his shoulder, Miranda saw the head was printed with the number three. Approaching the corresponding door at the end of the hall, Colin unlocked it and allowed Miranda to step inside.

Her heart beat a frantic rhythm against her ribcage. A combination of the aphrodisiacs and the anticipation of the moment made her lightheaded. She felt unanchored from reality. The entire situation was steeped in the ethereal eroticism of a wet dream, and she allowed herself to drift along its oneiric current.

The couple navigated through the darkened apartment to the bedroom. They shed their clothes and—in the fog of their passion—didn't hear them hit the floor. Miranda imagined that they had simply vanished before reaching the polished hardwood. They fell into bed, their bodies warm and damp on the crisp sheets. They made love silently, as though someone were listening. Panting was the only sound that broke the silence.

Then Colin spoke. "I don't want to lose you," he said over and over into her hair.

Miranda reached around and held him. You do care, after all, she thought, though she could not remember the specific exchange that inspired her epiphany.

Under their lips and hands, flesh shifted, stretched, and remoulded into something distinctly inhuman. The scent and taste of the worms reached their nostrils, and their tongues came alive with a host of flavours and impressions—the dinner they had consumed that evening, meals they enjoyed decades past, the lips and excretions of long lost lovers. And with these impressions, waves of pleasure—synchronized to the rhythm of their lovemaking—crashed through their bodies. Their flesh heaved into new shapes and configurations. Limbs readjusted to more effectively grasp and caress. Lips widened and teeth retracted to enhance mouth-to-mouth contact. Soon there was nothing recognizably human on the mattress.

When they were finished, they fell asleep pressed tightly together, motionless except for stop-motion jerkiness as their bodies reverted to more recognizable forms. The sheets were soaked with sweat from the toil of their metamorphosis, and worms with vaguely human faces writhed in the wrinkles and folds, birthed from the union of their lovemaking. All night, they remained in an unconscious caress, unburdened by dreams.

She awoke sluggishly to drab, grey light filtered through the curtains. The sky portended rain. Weather of this type made her melancholy, dredging up memories of half-forgotten gloom and heartbreak. She turned to Colin, but his side of the bed was empty, the area shallowly indented, sweat-stained, and perfumed with the slightly cloying musk of his body. A single worm twitched on the pillow, where his head had lain. She stared at it for an indeterminate time, filled with a longing she was hard-pressed to translate into a communicable thought. Eventually, she crawled out of bed and shuffled into the bathroom. Flicking on the light switch, she scrutinized the new face staring back at her in the mirror.

Light brown hair, sharp cheekbones, striking green eyes. For the briefest second she remembered Jillian—her face, mannerisms—then it faded like mist on the bathroom mirror as she leaned in to inspect every jut of bone, every pore.

Her phone vibrated in the other room. She stepped into the kitchen, realizing for the first time that the apartment wasn't the same place she—or rather Miranda—returned to with Colin the previous night. It was smaller, more austere. Her cellphone lay on the compact dining table. She picked it up and opened the notification from the Chimera application. It was a message from someone named Kathryn. The woman who had once been Jillian, Miranda, and who now was someone else entirely, recognized this Kathryn from somewhere—and for some reason, the name Michael flickered on the periphery of her mind.

I don't want to lose you.

The voice in her memory was male, familiar.

She grinned. Perhaps someday her lover would return to her in his original form. In the meantime, she would continue her pilgrimage, loving in her various guises, relishing the mutability of her flesh and the chimeric shapes of her lover. And one day, perhaps soon, the rift between them would be mended.

She began to compose a message.

Church of the Chronically Ill

MY MOTHER STANDS UNDER THE DUSTY CEILING FIXTURE, PALE and cadaverous, a gummy smile pulling at the leather-tight skin of her cheeks. Bathed in incandescent orange like a third rate angel, she extends her hand and beckons with trembling fingers. I stand in painful increments, using my chair as leverage, and shuffle toward the podium. The crowded basement resounds with the discordant clapping of the other Church members.

She welcomes me in a fragile embrace. *You look so handsome*, she whispers and kisses my cheek. When I pull away, the glow of the ceiling lamp has expanded the dark circles under her eyes, turning the sockets into black pools, each with a dim speck of light. *Are you ready?* I nod. Holding my shoulders, she turns me around to face the room. Anxiously, I adjust the knot on my tie, which hangs loosely around my neck like an untightened noose.

The basement, with its yellow, cigarette-stained walls, has been outfitted for the occasion. The plastic chairs are filled with parishioners—all familiar, unhealthy faces. The garbage bags stapled to the window frames are still present, but the surrounding walls are now decorated with cardboard cutouts of cartoon animals with bandages and thermometers sticking out of their mouths—a menagerie stolen from countless Get Well cards. Above the snack table, with its wrinkled, plastic table-cloth, the word BIRTHDAY has been excised from a HAPPY

BIRTHDAY banner, replaced by hand cut cardboard letters reading DIAGNOSIS DAY.

What draws my attention the most, however, is a dessert tray with an opaque plastic dome. I believe my mother received it as a wedding present. Throughout my childhood and teenage years, it sat atop the kitchen cabinets, collecting dust, until it was brought down for birthdays and, more infrequently, occasions like today. It rises conspicuously above the bowls of snacks and towers of plates, watching me like some predator waiting to strike.

I know what it contains. I can almost taste it. My stomach flutters in nervous anticipation, my mouth waters. Its presence —so conspicuous it feels like a physical weight—marks the end of my existence as a healthy, prosperous young adult. At the thought, I am overcome with a confusing blend of fear and anticipation.

I take a deep breath through my nose—odors of mold and dampness—and let it out in a rush. As I begin to speak, my voice sounds strange, even to my own ears—softer, frail and slightly tremulous. It reminds me of my mother's feeble tone. *Thank you everyone for coming tonight,* I say, wringing my clammy hands together. *It means so much to see you on this*—I hesitate—*important day. As most of you know, my mother was blessed with a debilitating immune disorder when she was thirty-two years old. Her condition was hereditary, and I have since received her benediction.* The words come effortlessly, like an oft-recited prayer.

The parishioners break into another round of dissonant applause. *Thank you,* I mumble. *My symptoms manifested over a year ago—my immune system betrayed me, assaulting healthy cells and organs, leading to chronic pain, lethargy, and uncoordinated movement.* How many times have I spoken these words, to doctors, to family, to friend? These words have become my identity. *Now, after all this time, I have received a formal diagnosis.* More applause. *I would like to take this opportunity to thank my mother, who has given me this blessing, introduced me to the Church, and taught me that I am stronger through my illness.* I finish with a humble nod, and the parishioners answer with another spate of applause. The sound rings unpleasantly in my ears.

Among the crowd, I pick out Jonah Berringer, the hemophiliac. Beside him, Anne McKee—in the latter stages of leukemia—weakly claps her hands together. Near the back of the congregation, Peter Cordello and his daughter, Becca—both afflicted with a rare genetic disorder—lean into one another and beam in my direction. I remember each of their diagnosis day celebrations. Becca's was the latest. A warm, intimate affair her father had eagerly anticipated since the moment he conceived Becca with another member of the Church, now deceased. Their union was engineered by the Church with the sole intent of producing an heir to Peter's genetic blessing. Unlike myself—diagnosed at sixteen—all Becca knew was illness.

My ruminations are cut short when my mother stifles a sob and pulls me in for another embrace. She smells of sweat and disinfectant. *I am so proud of you*, she says. *Our family is stronger than ever. United in sickness*. A chair squeaks in the sea of parishioners. The founder of the Church, Dr. Gregory Thornton, rises like a corpse from a long-dug grave. His cane, crafted from wood and animal bone, sways in his grip. The few patches of thin, silver hair on his mottled scalp hang like cobwebs over his brow and ears. He smiles—his teeth mostly rotted away—at my mother and me, and we advance toward him. His lips on my forehead are dry and brittle. We take a seat as our leader limps toward the podium, cane clicking on the laminate floor.

Good afternoon, my fellow afflicted, he intones. *Good afternoon Dr. Thornton*, we answer in one voice. *Today*, he continues, *we celebrate the diagnosis of one of our newest members, Cameron Beatty. Cameron has inherited the blessing of his mother, Eleanor, and we now officially welcome him into the fold. Let us hang our heads and thank our biological benefactors for our good fortune.* I bow my head along with the other parishioners. Unlike them, however, I keep my eyes open, staring at my loose-fitting khakis and scuffed leather shoes. Shoes once belonging to my father. If the blessing had not consumed him, he would be sitting beside me now, bowing his head in appreciation. Even today, I'm uncertain how I feel about his passing. Is my father indeed a martyr, as the Church dictates, or is he simply dead, sickness—I mean, the blessing—only meaningful when it can thrive in living flesh? Either way, I miss him.

I remember his diagnosis day, more vividly than the others. The cancer had hollowed him out, whittling his features into sharp points and shadow-haunted grooves. Despite this, however, he was still smiling—the blessing coursing through his veins—a cluster of pale crumbs on the corner of his mouth. *It is delicious*, he said, laughing. Then, to the room, *exactly what I expect from my beautiful wife*. The air around him smelled of vanilla and a sickly sweet stench like rotting fruit. He barely had the energy to chew, or keep his eyes open.

Dr. Thornton breaks the silence. *Life is inherently meaningless*, he says—words familiar to everyone seated in the basement of his dilapidated bungalow. *The only constant is suffering. But suffering is hierarchical.* Several parishioners nod their heads and rub their hands together. *At the bottom of the hierarchy stand those who suffer through unsatisfying work conditions, poor finances, or interpersonal problems. At the pinnacle, resides mental or bodily illness. For, in a world defined by fear and suffering, illness gives you purpose. Illness makes you stronger.* The crowd gasps and claps quietly. It sounds like a flock of pigeons taking flight. *You become one of the chosen*, Dr. Thornton says. *Through the ravages of disease you discover the value of life. You are blessed. You are more privileged than your healthy brothers and sisters. You transcend through illness.* The parishioners erupt into a standing ovation, momentarily forgetting their infirmities to give praise to their shepherd.

My mother smiles in my direction as we stand and clap. She has long waited for this day, the day her son would attain enlightenment. I like to think I share her enthusiasm. But something is out of place. If chronic illness is the cure for fear and suffering, then why I am still afraid? Why is the pain coursing through my body a burden and not a source of ecstasy? Why do my thoughts keep returning to my father?

You are all familiar with the manifesto by now, says Dr. Thornton, *but it bears repeating as we usher Cameron into the fold. And speaking of Cameron, I want to point out that he is an aspiring poet.* Warmth rises into my face. I bite the inside of my cheek. *And, as we know, some of the best artists, both past and present, are blessed with disease. It is a wellspring for creative energy, a catalyst for genius. I am certain Cameron will not disappoint our expectations.* I taste blood on my tongue. *Anyway, that's enough gabbing from an old man. I am sure you are all eager to begin the celebration. But first, as tradition dictates, Eleanor has a surprise for our newest member.*

My mother groans into a standing position and slouches toward the snack table. She picks up the plastic dome—its time come at last—and carries it toward me. The flow of time grinds to a crawl. The dome grows closer, and closer, and my first instinct is to move away, but I am rooted to my seat. The other parishioners watch, as though entranced, as she places it on her now vacant chair and removes the dome to reveal a circular loaf of sweet bread. The Eucharist. Charred fingers creep up from the underside. The knife lying beside it at an angle throws back a warped reflection of my face. For a moment, no longer than a heartbeat, my image fades, replaced by the aspect of my father. *It is delicious*, he says, chewing with great difficulty. He coughs, spraying pale crumbs on his chin and chest. They sprout slender, multi-jointed legs and crawls up his face, swarming him, consuming him, turning his—

Doesn't it look delicious, my mother says. She made the bread early this morning, while I slept. As she blended the flour, sugar, vanilla, milk and yeast mixture, she added half a dozen capsules from an amber bottle—a homemade concoction from Dr. Thornton's personal stores. The capsules contained a high dose of immune accelerants indented to keep me in a state of physical dysfunction. I know this because all members of the Church are subject to a similar act of communion—like my mother and father before me. It is no secret. How else are we to benefit from the sanctifications of illness? Medical treatment is never an option.

I imagine my mother kneading the dough, breathing hard from the effort. Perspiration glistens along her hairline. She pauses several times to flex her fingers and massage the swollen joints. Over time, the capsules disappear, swallowed and dissolved by the dough like they were never there at all. My mother then places the dough into a pan and slides it into the oven. She leaves the interior light on and watches it rise, feeling the heat from the viewing window palm and caress her face.

Now, using her hands, my mother tears off a generous fragment from the finished product. Dr. Thornton appears with a paper plate, and my mother carefully lifts the piece of bread onto it, smiling all the while. I take the fork Dr. Thornton holds out to me, and with my other hand accept the piece of bread from my mother. It is heavier than I expected. I smell yeast and, though I know it is not possible, a hint of something sharp and medicinal. I glance at my mother and Dr. Thornton. *Thank you both, for everything*, I say. My gaze returns to the bread in my lap, and beyond to my scuffed leather shoes—my father's shoes.

Ignore the fear. I am blessed. I have transcended through illness.

I cut off a piece with my fork, lift it to my mouth, and take a bite. My senses are overcome with a soft-textured sweetness and a tang of sweetness. It melts on my tongue, and I take another bite. *It is delicious*, I say. And around me, the room comes alive with eager applause.

THE LIVING COLUMN

1

LELAND MASS TRUDGED INTO HIS HOTEL ROOM IN THE GREY MUTE
hours of pre-dawn. Jet-lagged, hungry, and in desperate need of
a bowel movement, he dropped his suitcase near the door and
hurried into the washroom. He slapped the wall for the light
switch, but found only an irregular sea of plaster. Muttering
obscenities, he unbuckled his belt, shuffled into the dark, and
lowered his bulk onto the vague, dimly gleaming outline of the
toilet. He sighed as his airline breakfast of dry scrambled eggs
and overcooked sausage hit the water with a prolonged splash.
Once relieved, he remained seated—folded like a severed mari-
onette—exhausted from his travels.

He had set out more than twenty-four hours ago, when the
sun had yet to rise and his face was still swollen with sleep. His
itinerary consisted of a two-hour layover, an unexpected delay,
and a turbulent trans-oceanic flight that lasted throughout the
night. Over the course of this ordeal, he was jostled awake
several times—oily with sweat and tangled in nightmares—and
whenever he glanced out the window, he perceived nothing but
dense and formless darkness. Half asleep and addled by dreams,
he had the uncanny impression the darkness was alive,
enveloping the aircraft with ravenous, predatory awareness.

On reaching his destination, his subsequent journey from the airport to the hotel was mired in a fugue of exhaustion and cultural whiplash. He recalled a discordant chorus of voices speaking in a foreign tongue; a bright vascular network of neon outside a car window beaded with rain, and a smell like dark chocolate mixed with gasoline.

At some point, when the cab was snarled in traffic, the driver had turned to stare at Leland through the safety partition. He was younger than Leland had expected. Collar-length black hair and an upper lip darkened by an anemic, adolescent moustache. His jaw worked for a moment, chewing something, then he spoke. The interaction that followed was—in hindsight—tainted with the murky surrealism of a dream, or drug-induced hallucination.

"Looking for distraction?"

Leland hesitated. "I'm here for business."

"Then you certainly need distraction," the driver said, lips drawing back from crooked, masticating teeth.

Leland returned the smile, albeit awkwardly.

"This is a good place to start." He slipped a card through a narrow slot in the partition.

Leland took it, examining both sides.

EXCITING COMPANIONSHIP
OUTCALL @ HOTEL
CALL & TXT

At the bottom was a local phone number. On the reverse side, a single message was scrawled in tight handwritten script: Fleisch für die Lebenden Säule. It was German—he could tell that much—but the only word he vaguely recognized was *fleisch*, the German word for flesh. An esoteric reference to the sex work advertised on the card, perhaps? He thanked the driver from the corner of his mouth and slipped the card into his wallet.

For as long as he could remember, Leland had been ambivalent about sex work. He neither supported nor decried its existence, but simply regarded it as an inoffensive and necessary part of society. Despite this, he had never commissioned someone for their services—despite his bachelorhood and frequent time travelling for work. In fact, he had been involuntarily celibate for over a year. The myriad prescription drugs coursing through his veins had tempered his desire and impaired his ability to reach arousal. He could not say whether he missed the intimacy of sex—on occasion he detected a flicker of loneliness deep within—but his thoughts were so muddled by depression, the search for carnal gratification was low on his list of priorities.

Later—at the hotel's front desk—while Leland passed his credit card to the clerk, the business card had slipped out, landing reverse-side-up on the polished wood between them. He stared at it dumbly, failing to recognize what it was—the German words scrambling the language center in his brain. When the truth dawned on him, warmth filled his cheeks, and his hand flashed out to retrieve the card. The clerk merely stared, betraying no hint of recognition or judgment. Once the card was safely tucked away again, she smiled and proceeded with the registration process. Leland relayed his information in the rusty tone of someone who had long been silent. His mouth was stale, his teeth mossy, and he experienced a surge of inadequacy as he made eye contact with the clerk. Her eyes were grey, like the sky that had begun to lighten when, later, he ascended in a mirror-walled elevator to his room on the fifth floor.

Now, slumped on the toilet, his thoughts oscillated between the episode with the clerk and his business meeting later that day. Between now and then, he had enough time for a quick nap and a shower. He reached for the toilet paper. And froze when he noticed something on the floor. His vision had adjusted somewhat to the gloom, and a thin dark line had delineated itself along the base of the bathtub. He extended his hand toward it, hesitated. It remained motionless. *Okay, so not alive.* He pinched it between thumb and forefinger—it was light and brittle as a piece of confetti—and brought it up to his face for a closer look.

It wasn't alive, but once belonged to something living. The shed skin—no, not skin—it was the molted exoskeleton of some kind of nymph or larva. The thing was pale, yellowish-brown, semi-transparent, and ridged in a manner that suggested segmentation. From end to end it was perhaps seven inches, and roughly one inch wide. One extremity was slightly wider, rounded and tapered to a point—the head, perhaps? He grimaced as he turned the thing over, examining it from multiple angles. He had no idea what it could have belonged to. All he knew was he did not want to find whatever had left it inside his bed.

He dropped the molt into the toilet, cleaned up, and strode into the main area. The room was Spartan, indistinguishable from the innumerable hotels Leland had visited over the years: cream-colored walls with a generic abstract print above the bed. A desk with a lamp and chair stood opposite, and the wall facing him held nothing but a single rectangular window. He approached it, squinting against the growing dawn. The view would have been just as unremarkable as the room itself, if it were not for the lone building in the middle distance.

The structure, which could be best described as a high-rise, was clad in sallow, grey brick. Dark streaks spilled from the rooftop, painting the façade with a pattern of vertical stripes, like rain spillage that never dried. The windows, cast in murky, tinted glad, were framed in irregular red splotches Leland assumed to be colored brick or siding. However, when he squinted, he realized the substance wasn't part of the building's structural intent, but some form of crimson mold or moss. It likely grew there over the years due to the heightened elevation and persistent rainfall. Whatever the reason, the effect was unsettling. The building gave the impression of something long-dead—old, coagulated blood rimming its myriad sightless eyes.

Behind it, mountains—emerald with dense rainforest—faded into an uncertainty of mist and low-lying clouds. There were no hints of civilization beyond; it was as though the lone high rise was the last bulwark between tangible reality and an ephemeral otherworld.

His breath clouded the glass, obscuring his view of the building. He drew back when he realized how close he had moved to the window. Now, a couple paces away, he watched as his breath shrank to a pinpoint, a ghostly blemish over the structure in the distance. He couldn't explain it, but there was something about the high rise that both disturbed and fascinated him. What purpose did it serve? Was it abandoned? Why did it emit such a mystifying aura?

Leland drew the curtains and turned to face the bed. He didn't have the time to dwell on the view outside his window. He had a meeting later that day, and desperately needed sleep. Stripping down to his underwear, he slid the covers away from the bed, ran his hand over the crisp, white sheets—ostensibly looking for worms—and crawled inside. Sleep found him with foreseeable swiftness. The moment he closed his eyes, the room spun, his awareness dulled, and dreams trickled in from the well of his subconscious. Memories of his travels—the darkness outside the plane; the rain-drenched, neon-lit streets; the pallid building outside—mingled with outlandish visions drawn from his sleep-deprived imagination: a woman with a too-wide head and elongated rictus; a barren hallway with humming fluorescents—*Is this what it looks like inside the building*, Leland wondered, semi-conscious—and finally a worm of impossible size undulating through the void of space. He floated along with it. And as it vanished into the immensity of the void, his consciousness faded along with it. And for the first time in this strange land, Leland Mass surrendered to sleep.

2

The hotel bar was modest but well stocked with a variety of liquors from around the world. Leland had just returned from his meeting in the city, and was seated on one of stools, savoring his third glass of spirits. The liquor coated his tongue in a sweet, vaguely aniseed flavor and his chest burned with a pleasant glow. The bartender—a short, gaunt man who somehow looked both old and young at the same time—was idly cleaning a glass as he stared at the television mounted near the ceiling. Onscreen, a camera tracked the erratic movements of a protest. Masked demonstrators fled the batons, tear gas, and riot shields of an encroaching line of military policemen. The screen was filled, for an instant, with the bruised and bloody visage of one of the protestors. He repeated the same foreign word over and over through broken teeth. Leland imagined it was a plea for mercy.

The bartender made a clicking sound with his tongue—whether it was disapproval at the violence or something else, Leland could not tell for sure. He turned and placed the newly polished glass on the bar—directly in front of a woman who had not been there moments before. Leland spun to face her. It was the hotel clerk. There was no mistaking those pale, grey eyes. He smiled, already feeling the effects of the alcohol. "Done work for the day?" he asked.

She tilted her head slightly, brow furrowed. "I'm sorry?" There was the hint of an accent in her speech, an interrogative lilt betraying her lack of familiarity with English.

Embarrassment warmed his face. "You are the clerk, aren't you?"

She shook her head.

Leland laughed humorlessly. "I'm sorry. I thought you were the woman from the front desk." *Great*, he thought, *now she probably thinks I'm racist.*

"No," she said. "Just a guest. Like yourself, I assume?"

"Yeah." He exhaled a frustrated breath. "I'm sorry. I didn't mean to come off as—"

"Please, stop apologizing," she said. And, after a pause where she was visible searching for the words, added: "I must have one of those faces."

Leland downed the remainder of his drink. "I suppose so," he said, and gritted his teeth at the burn.

He glanced in her direction again, sheepishly. There was no way he was mistaken. Both women were identical. The same shoulder-length, tousled black hair—those eyes of course—and an identical, tapered chin. The only difference was the blue dress the woman was wearing, while her counterpart at the front desk had worn a black, form-fitting suit. Perhaps his mind was so addled by jetlag, it was finding similarities were none existed. Whatever the case, his initial confusion and embarrassment was rapidly transmuting into a nagging sense of unease.

The bartender poured golden, syrupy liquor into the woman's glass. She sampled it delicately and replaced the tumbler beside the battered paperback on the bar top. Feeling he needed to steer the conversation away from the women's identity, Leland asked, "What are you reading?"

The woman grazed the cover with her fingertips, "It is a work of philosophy. The title translates—roughly—to *The Death Flower Blooms in Winter*."

"Sounds grim."

"Quite the opposite," she said. "It is a treatise on the achievement of universal peace."

"I can see how that would be appealing," Leland said, and his gaze wandered to the television again. Two policemen were kicking a fallen protestor. The young man attempted to cover his head with his hands, but the hard boots of the officers easily battered them aside, mashing lips, nose, and forehead. His blood was thick and dark on the pavement.

Leland stared into his glass, the overhead lights undulating on the surface of the amber liquid. A sharp melancholy had abruptly pierced his drug-induced apathy. *Maybe I shouldn't be drinking so much*. The thought prodded him gently, carrying with a warning his doctor had issued about mixing antidepressants with alcohol. *We don't want to repeat what happened last winter*, he had said during one of their follow-up visits. Leland smothered the memory before it could resurface.

The woman looked at the television. Lowered her eyes again, regretfully, and focused instead on the cover of her book: a flower with skull-shaped petals emerging from a crust of snow.

"It is happening everywhere," she said, her voice barely raised above a whisper.

"Yeah," Leland said. He finished his drink. "The world is falling apart."

The woman gestured to the bartender. He moved to refill Leland's glass. Leland considered declining the offer—his conscience certainly protested—but to outside observers he simply watched the bartender work. Before he knew it, he had raised the replenished glass to his lips, inhaled its vapors, and poured the biting liquid down his throat.

He sensed the woman's eyes on him. When he replaced his glass on the bar top—repressing a cough—he noticed his hand was shaking. His uneasiness, which had lessened to dull throb throughout their conversation, was steadily creeping back.

"Are you all right?" she asked, staring into him with those grey eyes.

He hesitated, cleared his throat. "Yeah. I'm fine."

Whatever else he had intended to say evaporated from his awareness. He glanced around the bar as though searching for his train of thought. Everything was out of focus, the lights too bright. He blinked significantly, reached for his drink. A loud shattering and wetness down his leg. He gasped, made to slide off his stool, to help, to clean up his mess, but a hand—lithe-fingered and warm—pressed against the small of his back, arresting his movement.

"Are you okay, sir?"

The bartender glared at him through a fog of alcohol. Leland rolled his head to one side, seeing the woman—the clerk…it had to be, goddamnit—arm extended and supporting his back. Her expression was ambiguous. Leland sensed no warmth, no concern, only an odd sort of curiosity.

"I think it might be best if the gentleman returned to his room."

"I will assist him," the woman said. And to Leland, "What is your room number?"

What followed, Leland only recalled in a fleeting, discon-nected slideshow of images and impressions. The journey along the hallway from the bar; the soft *ding* of the elevator as it reached the ground floor; standing in a cramped space surrounded by dozens of strangers with smeared, vaguely familiar faces. Then they were inside his room, and though the only window framed nothing but darkness he sensed the high rise like a physical weight, pressing against his body, wrapping feelers around his skull. In his mind's eye, one of the windows erupted in sickly yellow illumination. Framed in the light: a tall silhouette with a too-wide face. And like the building itself—unseen but psychically intrusive—Leland knew that she was grinning...the unnaturally long rictus filled dozens of stubby, yellow teeth.

SOME TIME LATER, normal perception resumed, and Leland roused to find himself sprawled on the bed. The woman removed his shoes and placed them carefully in one corner of the room. The mattress shifted and bed sheets rustled as she climbed in beside him, hooking one leg over his hip. Her body emitted a heat fragrant with sweat and jasmine. Leland stared at the flat, white expanse of the ceiling, too tired, too drunk, to feel inadequate before this unexpected display of affection.

The woman leaned closer, her lips almost touching his earlobe. Her mouth clicked as she opened her lips to speak. "Fleisch für die Lebenden Säule."

Leland was not surprised to hear her utter those words. Some part of him had always known there was something unusual about the woman. First she had stolen the likeness of the clerk, and now she professed knowledge of a German phrase that—until now—had no connection to her whatsoever.

"What does it mean?" Leland said.

"Flesh for the Living Column."

"What's the Living Column?"

"I will show you. But not now."

She touched his chest, gently massaged his solar plexus.

"How do you know that phrase? How did you know I would recognize it?"

"It is from *The Death Flower Blooms in Winter.* As for the

answer to your second question, you displayed the calling card at the front desk."

"It was an accident," Leland said. "It fell out of my wallet."

"There are no accidents. The driver of that taxi knew to give you the card. And the card made itself known to the clerk. It was how I was summoned."

"You're talking as though the business card were alive."

"Not alive, but part of a living network, working toward a vital goal."

Through his drunken haze, Leland flashed on the cover of the woman's book. "What? Universal peace?"

She said nothing, only moved closer, lips grazing his neck. Gooseflesh erupted down his arms and across his chest. She kissed the stubble-flecked skin of his throat, not urgently but with tenderness he did not expect. Her lips were thin, soft, and tacky with lipstick.

"There is sadness within you," she whispered.

Leland continued to stare at the ceiling. The memory he had worked to repress earlier that evening breached the surface of his subconscious. He remembered lying on his back in the living room of his one-bedroom apartment, staring at a similar, unremarkable ceiling, as paramedics milled and fretted about him. His mouth tasted bitter, metallic, a combination of sleeping pills and the frothy bile foaming from his nostrils and out between his lips. Despite the frenetic energy around him, he was at peace, enveloped in a shroud of near-death bliss. The anger, anxiety, and corrosive sadness that had been distorting his personality for over a year were finally a distant memory. He wanted to inhabit that feeling forever, bathe in it, drown in it. But the bliss was, unfortunately, short lived. The paramedics managed to stem the encroaching tide of death and drag him back into the harsh light of his current circumstances. Alone. Broken. Lost.

"What happened?" The woman asked. Her tone gentle, prompting.

The words slid out of him like pus from a lanced boil. He explained—in slurring tones— how his family was no stranger to ill fortune. "It's like we're cursed," he said. "I don't know when it started, but the first incident I was aware of happened when I was eight. My grandmother tried to drown my little sister in the bathtub. I don't know what stopped her, but afterwards she claimed to have no memory of the incident. My sister lived to see another day, but just over a year ago, Death—denied his first attempt—paid her another visit. And this time, he got what he wanted. At the height of a weeklong manic episode, she walked into traffic on the highway. She was torn apart, crushed, and dragged until every trace of familiarity—everything that made my sister my sister—was gone. My mother couldn't handle the grief and ate an entire prescription worth of sleeping pills. Devastated by his losses, my father disappeared. I imagine that he crawled somewhere remote, like an animal going somewhere remote to die. And me, I tried to emulate my mother. Obviously it didn't go as planned. So now I've been losing myself in work and fistfuls of medication."

"You know you are not obligated to follow them," the woman said. "You can find help. You can heal."

"I know. I'm just tired," he said. "There comes a point when tragedy warps you so completely it becomes a challenge to interact with the rest of the world. Suffering is a deranged sculptor." He laughed humorlessly at the drunken metaphor. "And with the world on the brink, I can't stand to think that I'll be alone when it happens."

"You will not be alone."

She kissed Leland on the mouth, her tongue pushing past his lips, running slick, warm, and smooth against his own. She tasted clean, somewhat earthy. Though leaden, he managed to raise his arms to cup her face, pull her closer into him, his tongue driving deep.

As their passion increased, Leland worried he would be unable to perform—the alcohol further hampering his dysfunc-tion—but as the woman reached down and gripped him through his slacks, he was surprised to discover he was painfully hard. His cock throbbed against her palm, spasming faintly, the pres-sure of her touch coaxing out a bead of pre-seminal fluid.

They undressed, never drawing too far apart as the fabric fell away from their bodies, tangling in the bed sheets, sliding to the floor. Her skin was a deep olive hue, unadorned by tattoos, piercings, or scars. Leland filled his hands with her breasts, her nipples rigid beneath his fingers. She made soft moaning sounds deep in her throat, barely audible—sobbing carried on the wind. She climbed on top of him, reached down and teased the head of his cock against her vulva. Leland groaned, pulse fluttering in his throat and temples. His mouth grew dry as he slide inside her, feeling every inch of her slippery, corrugated flesh until the tight fist of his scrotum rested against her ass. His breath escaped in a long, unfettered exhalation.

Riding him, she touched his cheeks, slid her hands up into his hair, fingernails running along his scalp. Her hands travelled down his body, to the hollow above his right hip. Pressure —a dull cramp—formed under ministrations. Something was moving under the layers of fat and tissue. Clouded as he was by drink and lust, Leland hardly paid it heed. He was intent on the woman's expression, flushed but relaxed, inquisitive. She pressed his abdomen, hard and probing. But he felt no pain or discomfort. Instead, his flesh parted with a dry popping sound, like she had pierced a hard papier-mâché shell and not human skin. Leland allowed his gaze to travel down her body, where they joined, and lower still to the new orifice in his abdomen. Inside, a white, glistening mass pulsed and writhed. The woman sank her fingers into it and extracted a handful of limp strands.

Worms. Their bodies were vaguely segmented and slightly broader at one end. Leland recalled the molt he found in the washroom. Had a similar extraction happened in this room before? Was this a place of exorcism, a house of healing?

The woman raised the handful of worms to her face, and still rocking back and forth on Leland's erection, dropped them into her mouth. Their slender bodies burst between her molars, and black ichor dribbled down her lower lip, painting her chin with a series of vertical slashes.

As the worms perished, a weight lifted from Leland's shoulders. Warmth enveloped him, a warmth oddly similar to when he consumed the sleeping pills. Only now it carried with it the promise of resurrection, not death.

The woman continued to devour the worms, scooping out handful after handful, until his abdominal cavity was free of parasites. She then worked her way up his chest, opening him along the way, dissecting his sternum, parting his throat, until she reached his head, which burst in a bloodless eruption of worms and milky gestational fluid.

She leaned in, forcing him deeper, and buried her face into his ruptured skull, lapping worms into her mouth and chewing with series of cracking sound, moaning all the while.

Leland's breath quickened. Pressure mounted in his groin. His anxiety, fear, anger, and most all, his grief ebbed away. The final dregs trickled to nothing as an orgasm tore through his body. He exploded into her, screaming from the pleasure and the flood of emotional release.

In the afterglow, he was whole again—undamaged, unscarred —glistening with sweat and weeping openly against the woman's breast. She cradled him, kissing his forehead, whispering, "Now you're ready. It is time for you to join the Living Column."

3

Leland stood naked in the hallway outside his room. Beside him was the woman, her chin, neck, and breasts stained black with worm entrails. All was silent. No other guests were visible. Nor could any evidence of their presence be heard behind shuttered doors. It was though the odd, unclad couple was alone in the building, the world.

The woman held out her hand, and Leland took it. They followed the hallway to the elevator. It opened without prompting, their nudity multiplied *ad infinitum* in its glass compartment. The machinery whirred overhead as the elevator began its descent. Still gripping her hand, Leland glanced at the woman, the smile of the blissfully ignorant—the newly born—stretching almost painfully at the corners of his mouth.

"I never asked you your name," he said as the elevator shuddered to the lobby floor.

She regarded him placidly. The door remained closed as she allowed the silence to stretch into an uncertain interval. Was she searching her mind for an adequate answer? Finally, her lips parted and she said, "I do not have a name. Or I have many. None of which will provide you with the understanding you are seeking."

The moment she finished, the doors slid open, and for a moment—above her shoulder in one of the myriad reflections receding into the depths of the mirror—Leland perceived a figure. It was not a distortion of his own image. Nor did it belong to the woman. Rather, the apparition was tall—almost twice his own height—and clothed in a drab, loose-fitting gown. The legs were exposed mid-thigh, the feet bare. Its arms hung limp, abnormally elongated passed the knees where they bloomed into gnarled, crooked fingers. Lank, black hair—heavy and glistening with oil—framed a too-wide head. Black, porcine eyes were pushed deep into a visage the color of slate, and under them stretched a foot-long grin to accommodate the broad head. Crack, skin-flecked lips curtained a nauseating array of nubbed teeth.

The Wide-Faced Woman—a figure he now recalled from dreams—watched him from across an ocean of mirrors. Leland understood that, in ordinary circumstances, he would have been overcome by fear. However, he experienced nothing but humility. For this was a miracle he knew he would never truly understand. He had entered the hotel a broken man. And now he was renewed. He had no reason to fear his healer. As he stared, he focused on her teeth, and it came to him in a flash of intuition that they were made for crushing and grinding soft-bodied prey —the teeth of a worm eater.

The woman stepped forward to exit the elevator and her innumerable reflections churned in a disorienting kaleidoscope of movement. One of them passed in front of the Wide-Faced Woman, erasing the apparition like a stain rubbed from the surface of the glass.

As LELAND and the woman passed through the lobby a series of urgent gasps drew their attention to the front desk. The clerk leaned against the wall, skirt bunched around her ankles, her chaste, white underwear snagged at the knee. Her face was a deep shade of red, eyes glassy with lust as she drove a finger deep into her swollen cunt.

As he watched, Leland understood, as in a dream, that an erotic pall had permeated the building. Almost as though the potency of his latter passions had broken the constraints of the flesh and carried through the halls like an intoxicating fume.

The clerk looked up and as aspect of confused horror overtook her lust as she noticed the woman standing beside Leland —the woman appropriating her face. Her astonishment was short-lived, however, for the needs of her body overrode all other reason. She continued to finger herself until an orgasm trembled the flesh of her thighs, and warm, terror-induced urine pattered alongside her come onto the hardwood floor.

The automatic doors droned open, and the couple moved on into the balmy night. The air was heavy with moisture: a warm, wet tongue lapping sensuously at their exposed flesh. The wind carried the perfume of ferns and the heady scent of hemlock. And woven among these smells was something else, something both familiar and ambiguous—a carnal aroma, a miasma of sweat and secret places. As they rounded the hotel, it grew ever more pervasive.

Leland knew where they were headed before they had completed their circumvention of the building. The parking lot transitioned to packed earth and, further on, sloped into a gentle incline furred with grass and weeds. Beyond that, the earth gave way sharply—a ragged, uneven plunge into the jungle below. Standing on the brink, the couple stared out over an expanse of emerald darkness, the tops of trees flecked with silver-blue moonlight. And when Leland craned his neck, he saw what he had been anticipating all along.

The high rise visible from his room window stood bathed in the excretions of the moon. As before, the windows, rimmed with moss like bloodstained orifices, stared out blackly, seeing nothing. The light shimmering along its edges and planes created the illusion of movement, as though the structure were composed of countless moving bodies, writhing and twitching in an effort to sustain the integrity of the structure.

Leland blinked and the illusion passed from his mind. All that remained was old brick and moonlight. "What is that place?" he asked the woman.

"Place?" She sounded genuinely confused.

He pointed. "The high rise."

"You see a building?" A smile crooked the corner of her mouth.

Leland froze, unable to respond as a new dread convulsed through his body. Her question had jarred loose a fundamental support in his mind. *Everything you know is nothing but a thin membrane over something unfathomable.* A sublime horror threatened to supersede the dread, but Leland managed to tamp it down through sheer force of will. When his existential paralysis abated, he inspected the building once again, and initially he could not make sense of what stood before him.

It was an intricate structure—a living mountain—comprised of nude men and women lashed together with rope. No, not rope. The tethering was pale white and pulsing with life. Worms. Similar to the breed extracted from his body. Only this species spanned lengths in excess of three meters. The longer Leland stared, the more it became apparent the structure was not merely vertical, but spread out over a mile through the jungle—a vast, undulating network of copulating bodies. A living column. Ecstatic moans and cries of pleasure came to him over the wind. And the carnal perfume he had detected earlier had attained its olfactory peak. The smell was like a living thing, crawling down his throat and nostrils, taking root in his stomach and lungs. He coughed and tears sprang to his eyes. His mind bowed under the immensity, the sheer divinity, of this cathedral of flesh and lust.

The woman held out a demonstrative hand. "Pain. Grief.

Anger. These are the prayers that have drawn these lost souls together. People very much like you. And sex is the magick that will allow us to depart this broken world. To finally find peace. Will you join us, Leland?"

Leland allowed his mind to turn away from the godhead, focusing instead on his family. They were no longer here to tell him, but he knew they would want him to find happiness. His depression, attempted suicide, and subsequent existence in a fog of medicated delirium, would only cause them pain. There was nothing for him here anymore. He had been unable to find happiness anywhere in the world. His travels had amounted to little more than aimless wandering. And now a solution beyond his wildest imagining had made itself known. He would be a fool to brush it aside. To deny a power that reached halfway across to world to offer him solace. The Living Column was the embodiment of his salvation.

He took a deep breath, smiled at the woman. "Will you be coming with me?"

She nodded. "You will not be alone. I promised you."

He took her hand and they descended together into the jungle.

THE HUMAN SCAFFOLDING of the Living Column was arranged in an endless tableau of sexual positions. Tongues lapped vulvas and nipples; lips—engorged with blood—ran the lengths of swollen, sputtering cocks. Hands moved over soft flesh, squeezing, raking with nails, and caressing the globes of breasts and buttocks. The worms moved through these networks of fornication, stopping occasionally to suckle the emissions drying on thighs or in a tangle of pubic hair. Nothing was still about the structure. The movement was electric, a passion hitherto unknown to human experience. Leland was immediately drunk on it.

The woman lead him to the base of the Column and—on instinct—one of the worms slithered down, coiled under his armpits and raised him into the structure. He was held securely, his back to a young blonde, her skin luminous with perspiration. She let out little panting sounds as a darker haired woman—at least twice her age—thrust her tongue deep into her cunt. She ejaculated violently, spraying the other bodies erected about her. The worm tethered around her midsection twisted around to taste a stray droplet of her fluids.

Leland watched as the woman ascended to take her place beside him. She immediately drew him close and kissed him on the mouth. Within seconds, he was hard and she reached down to slip him inside her. They fucked passionately in a galaxy of fornicating flesh, becoming one with the Column. Leland could feel its energy pulsing in the veins of his cock, in the rapid pulse at his throat. His ecstasy was beyond description.

Thunder in the distance—the splinter and crash of felled trees—drew his attention momentarily away from his partner. The woman pulled his lips back against her own and spoke into his open mouth. "It's happening," she said, her voice thin with orgasm. A tremor travelled the length of the Column. The human scaffolding moaned in one voice. A second more violent tremor jostled Leland so violently he almost head-butted the woman. It did little to deter his hunger, however. He drove himself deeper into her, his testicles drawing tight against his body. He came as the weightlessness overcame his body.

The Living Column stirred in sluggish eddies, snapping trees, and damming a river deeper in the jungle. Roused further from its slumber, it raised the front section of its bulk toward the moon—fifty feet, a hundred, three hundred—until observers a hundred miles away completely lost sight of the celestial body. The Column lingered in that position for several minutes, finding its bearings, scenting the air like a reared serpent. Finally, an immense tremor rocked the Column and the air resounded with a bang louder the detonation of a nuclear bomb. All the windows in the hotel shattered simultaneously. And with that, the Living Column took flight, carrying Leland Mass and his kin, into the silver-blue night.

"123. And the broken shall find salvation in the realms beyond...

151. Universal peace comes later, when the Living Column returns...

158. The Worm that devours the World."

— FROM *THE DEATH FLOWER BLOOMS IN WINTER*

GLITTERATI GUIGNOL

ACT ONE

Enter CANDACE and the SENATOR

Candace wiped the Senator's blood from her face and shoved his body behind one of the mansion's innumerable mini-bars. His head lolled at an unnatural angle, throat halfway slit and pumping dark, cholesterol-rich blood. The paring knife she'd used to open his jugular protruded from one eye socket, the curved blade having just performed an indelicate lobotomy. His arms twitched, the fingers wriggling inches away from his shrinking erection. His lips opened and closed like he was trying to say something but couldn't find the words. He looked old, shriveled—pathetic.

Candace spat on his dinner jacket, grabbed his drink from the bar top—Jack on the rocks—and knocked it back in one swallow. The burn peeled the lips from her teeth and she hurled the glass—which shattered brightly—into a corner of the room.

The old man had attacked her while she was searching the minibar for salvage. She had been in the middle of filling her purse with bar limes, celery salt, and several books of matches, when he staggered into the room, shirt open, belt unbuckled, and reeking of booze. He pinned her against the bar, slurring something about making the most of the time they had together before they were inevitably eaten and killed. "The world is over, you little brat. Just shut up and take it. It'll be fun," he'd said. As he clumsily lowered his pants, Candace drew the paring knife from her back pocket. The Senator had farted explosively when she plunged it into the flabby skin of his throat. The smell was monumental—a rancid, diabetic stench interwove with the sharp miasma of liquor. He staggered back, gingerly fingering the wound.

"D-David," he groaned, turning the name into a pitiful imploration.

"Fuck David," Candace had replied—the billionaire's name like bitter vomit on her tongue—and drove the knife into the Senator's brain.

NOW, as she stared at his corpse, something in her abdomen shifted with serpentine fluidity. It moved under the fabric of her top, pushing up against the skin from the inside. She groaned, double over, tried to control her breathing. *Let me out.* The voice slithered from her entrails into her brain. *I can help you. Let me free.* The mass had grown in the past few days—how long had she trapped on this fucking island, anyway? Three days? Four? A week? She couldn't remember. Whatever the case, she had barely noticed the mass after the bat with the baleen mouth had implanted it inside her body. But now, however many days later, the fact of its existence was inescapable.

What had the bat thing done to her exactly? Laid its eggs in her stomach like a carrion fly or an alien in some science fiction B-movie? She supposed it was possible. Nothing was outside the realm of conjecture—not after what happened, happened.

That was three days ago. She remembered now.

Three days of scavenging, hiding and running from the lust-starved and monstrosities so unimaginable, her mind strained under the mere contemplation of their existence. She hoped—

oh god she hoped—that once she was free of this place—this nightmare—that doctors would be able to remove whatever writhed inside her. All she wanted was to be back in her apartment. Behind a locked door. Curled up in bed. A record playing softly in the other room. The mental picture made her vision so hazy and she blinked the tears away. She certainly wasn't getting any closer to that image by standing here with the corpse of the old man. She had to get back to her hideaway in the basement laundry quarters. Figure out how to kill David Hoffman and get the fuck off this island.

The motion inside her stopped, and the pain receded. She straightened, gingerly, sucked in a lungful of air and started moving. As she walked, wiping bloody hands on her pants—and still shaking from the adrenaline—she reflected how rapidly she had descended into survival mode. She supposed the hedonism and cruelty already present on the island—there even before the air grew porous and those monstrosities spilled through—had coaxed a primitive instinct from the reptilian depths of her subconscious. It disoriented her to consider that such a violent part of her had slumbered, unacknowledged, while she worked at the local homeless shelter, and later as a stewardess, pouring coffee for tired travelers and comforting those with flight anxiety. How could anyone function in society while a force of such magnitude drowsed, prepared to rise the second conditions veered into the extreme?

Shouldering her purse, she moved on tiptoe down the hall, her bare feet silent on the plush, carpeted floor. The walls were dark, paneled oak punctuated—at intervals—by photographs of David with various celebrities and politicians, models and millionaires. Seeing him among such affluence, grinning, clean-shaven, and wearing expensive clothes, Candace understood why young women flocked to him. Superficially, he promised maturity, wisdom, influence, inspiration, and the enticement of new experiences. But, in reality, he was the proverbial wolf in sheep's clothing, a handsome predator capable of destroying a life before the victim could even realize what was happening—a fucking monster.

IT HAD BEEN the promise of new experiences that lured Candace to David Hoffman's remote island sanctuary. She grew up in an impoverished home. Her family rarely strayed more than a few hours from the city for the rare summer vacation. It had always been her dream to see the world, to explore new countries. And so she decided to become an airline stewardess, travel the globe as a means to save for college tuition.

It was on a flight from Los Angeles to Tokyo where she met David. He liked to fly business class. It was humbling, he would tell her later, and she couldn't help but roll her eyes at the sentiment now. While serving him dinner and a drink, he had invited her to his private island with the pretext of networking and a "party unlike anything she had ever experienced." Thoroughly entrenched in the You Only Live Once mentality of her generation, she graciously accepted the invitation. And he was right about the party— of course—but not the way that he had intended.

A week later, the world ended...

Candace was alone with David in the "massage room" when it happened. They sat together on a white leather couch. Music —some alternative indie band—played from a speaker near the ceiling. The air smelled of incense and massage oil.

"What do you think of the place?" David said, gesturing expansively.

"It's—" Candace hesitated. She wrung sweaty hands together in her lap. "A lot."

David laughed, flashing his straight, white teeth. Candace was unsure if they were real or veneers. He combed fingers through his voluminous, silver-flecked hair—a gesture somehow both casual and practiced—and shifted so his knees pointed in her direction.

"Yeah, it's a little ostentatious. But, c'mon, you can't tell me that you're not drawn to the idea of owning a mansion on a island. A smart, cultured woman like yourself." He touched her knee. "You can lounge on the beach all day. Throw parties for your friends."

"And slowly go mad as rain whips the windows and wolves howl in the night."

"This is the Virgin Islands," David said, seriously. "There aren't any wolves."

"I know," Candace said, smiling awkwardly.

The leather creaked under his weight as he leaned in, cupping her cheek. Candace watched—numb with shock—as his eyes closed and his lips puckered into a wet, pinched orifice. She started to pull away, but his fingers tightened around her ear, a clump of air snagging painfully between his knuckles. He twisted her ear like an old schoolmarm and pulled her toward his lips. The action was so unexpected and cruelly absurd, it shocked her into immobility, all the strength draining from her body.

"You like this," David whispered against her mouth. Whether he was trying to convince Candace or himself, she couldn't tell. He kissed her again. "You're so beautiful."

His hand moved up her leg and forced its way into her crotch. Just as his fingers brushed her pubic mound, a ringing started in her ears. David must have heard it too, for he flailed back, clasping the sides of his head. "What the *fuck*? What did you do to me?"

Candace pushed herself away, crab walked backward across the couch. One heels caught on the corner of the coffee table and she collapsed onto the floor. The ringing increased in volume, and she pressed her hands over her ears, groaning from the discomfort. It continued for several long, agonizing moments. Then silence. Her ears popped as though she were ascending in an airplane, and the window overlooking the ocean exploded in a brilliant shower of glass. Fragments struck her back and shoulders, snared in the curls of her hair. Something warm and wet trickled down her neck. She crawled to the opposite corner of the room, blood pattering to the floor from her forehead and scalp. The fat red drops on the white floor made her dizzy.

Ohgodohshitwhatthefuckishappening?

Somewhere behind her, David groaned and swore. Glass crunched as he got to his feet and staggered to the window. "Jesus fucking Christ," he breathed. "Did we get nuked or something?" Silence for a beat. Then a scream. Candace rolled over in time to see something huge and black swoop through the empty window frame and fall upon David, whose screams had reached a pitch she didn't think possible for human vocal cords.

She was unable to see the creature devour David Hoffman's face, but she heard it: a wet crunch followed by a peeling sound like sweaty skin released from warm leather.

When it was finished with the billionaire, it crawled to her on folded wings. Huge, pointed ears turned this way and that and the bottom half of its head was a fan of rigid baleen. Candace closed her eyes as it reached her, mentally preparing herself for death—if one could do such a thing—and yelped as the creature pushed something sharp into her abdomen.

When she opened her eyes, it was gone, the wound on her stomach had clotted over with an amber honey-like substance, and she was throttled by the understanding that her perception of the world and its mechanisms had been forever altered.

ACT TWO

Enter Candace, the Movie Star, and the Lawyer

The stairs to the basement—and relative safety—were close now. She was so eager to return to her makeshift encampment she neglected to peer around the corner into the adjoining corridor—to check for monsters or David's subjects—as was her custom. When she rounded the bend, she collided bodily with another person. Staggering back, she drew the blood-slick paring knife. It was the Movie Star. Beside and slightly behind him stood the Lawyer. The Movie Star chuckled, "Well, my man," he said over his shoulder to his companion. "Looks like the Slut Scavenger Hunt is over."

"Well, fuck me," David said. He sounded strange. Like he spoke with his lips pulled away from his teeth. "You found her. The one that got away."

He laughed and it was a horrible, dry, throaty sound.

Candace spat a mouthful of blood. Her eyes were nearly swollen shut and dried gore gummed the lower half of her face. "I'm going to kill you, you piece of shit," she said, not sounding like herself either—but more nasal and husky.

"Give me a break," David said. "No one is killing anyone. We're having fucking party."

"What do you want me to do with her?" asked the Movie Star.

"Whatever the fuck you want. *After* I'm done with her."

He jumped out of his throne, his erection swaying like a metronome needle. He danced a jig up to Candace and jabbed the head of the dildo into her abdomen. "We were in the middle of something... BEFORE WE WERE RUDELY INTERRUPT-ED!" David screamed that last part to the ceiling, a drunken, deranged challenge.

Alcohol fumes wafted from his sweat-slimed skin. And now that she was closer, Candace discerned a necklace of blood that trickled out from under his mask. She thought again of the fleshless skull. He grabbed hold of her shoulders and she winced.

"You will like this, Candace," he said, his eyes huge and unblinking through the holes in the mask. "You will like this very much."

Let me out. I can help you. Set me free.

The thing in her abdomen twisted violently. The pain almost knocked her over. She groaned and David took a tentative step back. To the Movie Star, he said, "Jesus. What did you do to her?"

The Movie Star shrugged. "Shot her." And when disbelief overtook David's features, he quickly added: "In the shoulder. She's fine."

Let me out. Set me freeeeeeeeeeeee, the voice pleased. Then: *I will save you.*

She had no choice now. Why turn down help when it was offered? Even if the benefactor wasn't human.

"I set you free," she said out loud.

David tilted his head inquisitively. "Come again?"

Her stomach exploded in a flash of agony so exquisite it was like an orgasm. Perhaps the thing living inside her had filled her veins with a potent narcotic? Her perception was altered as well: colors were brighter, more vivid; David left tracers in the air as he staggered back, blood-flecked and horrified. She looked down in slow motion. Her belly was gone. Torn fabric hung over a porthole into a starry void. *Thank you*, the voice whispered. Candace widened the portal with her hands and the procession emerged, crawling free to be born into the vastness of the ballroom. There were creatures of every size and description, things without recognizable traits, others a chimerical mishmash of disparate elements. And as they poured loose, Candace understood that—like herself—they had been imprisoned in their island void at the furthest reaches of existence. And now, after millennia of hunger and isolation, they were finally free. Joy unlike any she had experienced before flooded her system. She glanced around the room, idiotic in her bliss, and watched as the monsters devoured the members of David's court, ripping them open to drink their insides, tearing a limb to strip away the sweat-glazed flesh. The decadents screamed, and wept and begged, and to Candace it was like a symphony reaching its moment of catharsis. She held out her arms to embrace the scene and smiled.

David scrambled away, grabbing onto one of the legs of his throne as if that could save him. He had a moment to reflect how he had been largely ignored by this hellish invasion, until the bat with the baleen mouth landed in front of him—the thing that'd eaten his face and sent his already fragile psyche into madness.

"No, get away." David screamed, kicking out at the thing with his skinny, naked legs.

It advanced on him undeterred. Leaned forward to feast on his face and bumped into the mask. Using the clawed toe of one wing, it swung down at the plaster, again and again, until it crumpled dryly, spilling down the sides of David's disfigured head. It wasn't a bare skull, exactly, but close enough. Muscle and sinew riddled with infection stretched over glistening bone. His mouth—lipless—was a permanent grinning rictus. Once the shell had been broken, and the edible core exposed, the bat thing leaned in and clamped down on the petty remains of David's face. His legs and arms flailed. There was a hollow crunch as the front of his skull gave way. The bat thing slurped his brain and the coral flesh of his nasal cavity. David Hoffman, as crude as ever, shit himself as he died.

Candace waved her arms in the air to the symphony that played on in her drugged mind. The carnage continued unabated around her, and before she knew it, the marble floor was flooded with two inches of blood, and her body was likewise painted with it. She rubbed it into the lines of her face, against her lips, laughing all the while.

After a time, the frantic motion had abated and the symphony had progressed to a gentle coda. The prisoners were feasting, filling their impoverished stomachs, and Candace weaved—dancing between them. When she reached David, mulched at the base of his throne, she held out her hand as though to help whatever was left to him to his feet—and stuck out her middle finger. "I told you I would kill you," she said in a slurring tone.

Turning, she found the bat with the baleen mouth standing on its hind legs before of her. It regarded her for a moment, without eyes, its ears twitching, and bowed its head. The gesture was slight but easily recognizable. Candace happily bowed in return, placing one hand over her breast. *Thank you*, the voice in her head said again.

"My pleasure," she said.

We will protect you. We will take you away from here.

"I'm ready." She fanned out her arms.

The bat with the baleen mouth approached, nuzzled itself

against her cheek, moved behind her, and lifted her from the ground, flapping its enormous wings. Ripples formed in lake of blood. Her feet dangled above the ground, higher and higher—her toes dripping red—until she was nearly touching the ceiling. There was a small window up there. Her way out. When she looked down, Candace saw her reflection as though in a crimson mirror. With the bat thing holding her from behind, she looked for all the world like she had wings.

Exit CANDACE

CURTAIN

Nostalgia Night at the Snuff Palace

1

THERE WERE FOUR OF THEM—BRIAN, KATY, ARMAAN, AND GEOFF —trudging through the ruins of the city like living nuclear shadows. Winter garments caked with ash and grime hung in tatters over their emaciated frames. Exhaustion chiseled deep lines their faces, and blue, bleeding lips whispered lyrics to half-forgotten songs—a futile attempt to soften the horror of their surroundings. They were close now. Once they reached the heart of the city, and the miraculously still-standing movie palace, their pilgrimage would be complete.

Cresting a hill formed by shattered concrete and rusted rebar, the pilgrims approached a ruined gas station and collapsed into the dirt. The metal canopy leaned at an angle, one end raised toward the sunless cauldron of the sky. Shadows congregated underneath, thick as pitch. With cautious glances, the pilgrims ensured they were a safe distance away. The darkness likely held the hungry, the desperate, or the deranged. Worse still, it could be concealing one of them—the so-called Carolith—their bodies sleek, unmoving, and indistinguishable from shadow. Unlike the threat of physical violence, there would be no chance of surviving an encounter with the Carolith. And so the pilgrims kept a wary distance, watchful in spite of their debility.

Geoff removed his backpack with painful, meticulous movements. The zipper had long since broken and the opening was held together with safety pins. He removed one of them with blistered fingers, reached inside, and removed a shapeless thing wrapped in soggy newspaper. A blurred headline hinted at a war remembered now as a distant, collective nightmare. The stink emanating from it was so powerful, so nauseating, it seemed to extend putrid, fecal-stained fingers into the nostrils and down the throats of the pilgrims. Despite their revulsion, saliva sprang into their mouths. They drew nearer as Geoff peeled away the newspaper membrane—matted fur oleaginous with brown, clotted blood, the bright flash of bone. It was so twisted out of shape, crushed, and filthy, none of them could tell what animal it was—violence had reshaped it into something new, something disturbingly abstract.

Brian reached into a pocket and withdrew his utility knife. Geoff held up one hand and gave his head a gentle shake. No need to blunt the blade, he relayed without words. To demonstrate, he simply pulled one of the creature's extremities. It came away without effort, trailing limp sinew, a trickle of dark fluid, and a single bloated maggot. Katy grabbed it as soon as it struck the earth and slapped it into her mouth. It burst between her cavity-laden teeth, splattering her tongue with cold, vaguely nutty slime. She swallowed rapturously, eyes closed, face raised toward the perpetually clouded sky.

Geoff proffered the limb to Armaan who took it eagerly, gnawing at whatever remained of the rancid meat. Everyone received a similar portion and the following minutes were loud with chewing, retching, and the occasional sob. When the pilgrims finished their meager ration, they huddled together for warmth. Katy unwrapped the blanket she wore as a cloak and shared it with the others. It abraded their frostbitten skin and stank of the long journey, but they all welcomed the little comfort it provided.

Each sunk into a shallow half-dreaming state, recalling the

world as it had been before the bombs had fallen. But their dream-memories were half-formed, pocked with holes and shrouded in haze. The images and impressions were tantalizing, but heart-wrenchingly out of reach. It was almost worse than having no memory of the past at all. But that would hopefully change once they reached the movie palace. Survivors made the journey from all corners of the shattered world to see images flashing on the palace's movie screen—rare images of the world as it had been before, images without holes or an obscuring haze. The pilgrims hoped with every shred of their beings that it would reinvigorate their memories and give them the much-needed strength to persevere in this unimaginable hell. Having lost everything and everyone but each other, it was the only thing left that gave them reason to live.

Their breath clouded the air as they hovered between vaguely pleasant dreams and a waking nightmare. Armaan was the first to twitch awake. He moaned and burst into wheezing sobs. The din woke the others and they drew closer still, sharing his anguish. Geoff brushed the hair from Armaan's face in an almost maternal gesture and kissed the corner of his mouth, tasting tears, ash, and sour breath. Armaan moved into the kiss, opening his mouth, their tongues coated in putrescence. Joining in what had recently become a morale boosting ritual, Katy cupped Brian's cheek and pulled him toward her lips. Trembling hands explored the other's body; ribs, hips, and collarbones tangible through layers of fabric. The pilgrims traded affections: belts clattered, zippers growled, skin slapped weakly against skin. Focus on the electric rub of flesh on flesh. The internal warmth of the body. Your partner's breath against your neck. Drown out the fear. We can't lose hope now—these statements passed through each of their minds as they brought the other to passionless, anemic climax.

Once finished, they lay together, shivering and exhausted under Katy's blanket. The wind lamented and in the distance, gunfire sounded. Muzzle flashes pulsed in the dust clouds smothering the highway. The display was perversely lulling, and soon the pilgrims succumbed to fitful sleep. This time, however, their dreams did not reach into a half-forgotten past, but rather centered on a single, shared image: a vast, reflective eye watching them from above. Or at least that is what they believed before they were struck by a bolt of lucid epiphany. It wasn't an eye at all, but a camera lens—though they could not discern who or what stood behind the apparatus. The camera hovered over their sleeping bodies, whirring mechanically, panning left and right with pornographic zeal. The air was filled with squelching, ripping sounds, and choked with the damp stench of the slaughterhouse.

When the pilgrims awoke, their mouths were full of blood, flesh was caught between their teeth, and one of their own was dead.

2

Geoff had been mutilated beyond recognition. Skull smashed, the contents fanned out in a crown of white, raw pink, and shimmering crimson. Among the detritus, several teeth and a single bloodshot eye were visible. It stared into an imprecise distance, seeing nothing. A fly crawled across the lead-grey iris. His body was likewise deformed. The chest had been crushed, near the sternum; stomach ripped open, loops of intestines trailing between his legs. His penis had been sawed off with a jagged instrument—probably a chunk of asphalt based on the black grit in the stump. Human teeth marks covered most of his body, and the muscles on his thighs and biceps had been stripped from the bone—likely eaten.

The pilgrims exchanged appalled glances. Blood covered their faces, chests, and hands. It had dried to a tacky reddish brown film. Unable to consider the implications of this tableau, Armaan grabbed his clothes and pulled them over his exposed skin, screaming all the while. His coat had been so heavily saturated with blood it froze into a bizarre, crumpled sculpture. He struck it against the ground to loosen the fabric, clumsily put it on. Following his lead, Brian and Katy grabbed their frosted garments and dressed.

"What happened?" Katy wailed. "What did we do?"

"It was a dream. We're still dreaming," Brian ranted.

"It couldn't have been us," Armaan said. He glanced toward the ruined gas station, stabbed a finger toward its blackest recess. "It was something in there." When he spoke again, his tone was low, almost a whisper. "The Carolith."

"Maybe they made us do it. They can do that, can't they?" Katy was sobbing, tears slicing tracks through the blood congealed on her face.

Brian simply stared at the corpse, reached numb fingers to his lips, his stomach. The fingers sank lower and he did something he had not done since childhood—he slipped one hand down the front of his pants and cupped his genitals. It was a nervous tick, a coping mechanism, totally unconscious until parents and schoolteachers told him to stop. He remembered their scolding tones as he followed the loops of Geoff's intestines with his eyes. A thin, white sheet of frost had formed over the corrugated flesh, giving it a surreal, artificial appearance.

"We can't stay here," Armaan said. "We're too close now."

"We need to bring him with us." Katy wailed, her words nearly incomprehensible.

"We already are," Brian spoke finally, his tone flat.

He turned and vomited his share of Geoff into the dirt. Blood, bits of masticated skin, and even hair was blended with the meager acid from his stomach. As soon as he was empty, the tears came, hot and stinging. He was not certain if they were the result of Geoff's passing, or the fact that he had just lost valuable, life saving calories.

"Fuck this," Armaan said. He grabbed Geoff's backpack, threw it over one shoulder. "Are you two coming, or am I leaving you here?"

Brian, hunched forward with his hands on his knees, spat, said weakly, "I'm coming."

Katy, still sobbing, shuffled over to Armaan and curled into his chest. He wrapped his free arm around her back, squeezed her against his body.

"We need to wash him off," Brian said, straightening.

Armaan considered the suggestion as he stared into Brian's cannibal mask. He shook his head. "Think of it as camouflage. Geoff can still protect us as we move deeper into the city. It'll only get more dangerous from here."

Brian groaned and Armaan thought he was going to throw up again, but he only leaned forward and let another glob of spit fall. When he moved closer to his companions, he gave Geoff's remains a wide berth. Armaan touched his face, trying to convey comfort with a glance, but realized the effect was probably lost through the layers of blood. He turned his attention instead over Brian's shoulder—at the wreckage of the gas station.

The darkness under the canopy shifted, seemed to breathe. For an instant, Armaan thought he could make out a vaguely human silhouette, black against black. And was that the whirring of an ancient camera? He pulled his gaze away.

"We need to get moving."

THE PILGRIMS TRUDGED DEEPER into the city, silent and guarded. As they neared the crippled skyscrapers of the financial district, they encountered the first people since leaving their tent city, three weeks ago. Travelers, like themselves, congregated toward the ruins, while others moved away, pulling makeshift rickshaws in quest of salvage. Every face was lined with misery; some were hidden under layers of filthy, bloodstained bandages; others had been distorted by some form of leprosy or cancer, skin turned a lumpy, ashen grey, hair missing save for the stray, bleached strand. Those who acknowledged the pilgrims swiftly looked away, those who did not gave them a respectable—or perhaps fearful—distance.

As they approached a collapsed, once-elevated highway, they encountered a disturbing scene. An uncountable number of bodies lined the pavement. Spools of nitrate film, partially burnt, had been threaded through their orifices, winding from anus to orbital socket, mouth to ear canal. The corpses were naked. On every stomach a different symbol was carved deep into the flesh —deep enough to expose the yellow layer of fatty tissue. The pilgrims did not recognize the symbols—they were unspeakably alien, a maze of twisting lines, dashes and curls. The only recurrent element was a single spiral tucked away somewhere in every etching. As Brian leaned forward to inspect the nitrate, Armaan grabbed his bicep and pulled him back.

"Don't look at it," he said. "It's not for us."

Armaan imagined holding the nitrate to the sky, seeing the images burned there, and screaming until he gargled blood and his carotid burst from the strain. For he knew not all films in this fallen world were considered equal. The symbols had made it apparent to him this gruesome scene was not the work of other humans, but the Carolith.

After the bombs fell, the Carolith emerged from the ruins and appropriated human art as their chosen form of expression, or perhaps communication. Their work appeared across the blasted landscape, and the theme was always the same: a marriage between filmmaking equipment and the human body. Though their method was apparent, the meaning behind these displays eluded the survivors. Armaan wondered whether these installations—celluloid threaded through flesh and processed with blood—were a method for the Carolith to consume cinematic media. As the thought entered his mind, he nearly burst into a fit of unhinged laughter. Before that could transpire, however, he dug his nails into his arm until he drew blood.

Brian looked at Armaan then back at the bodies. He stepped away. Katy moved beside him, arms wrapped around her chest. "There aren't any flies," she said, voice flattened by shock.

She was right. The bodies, aside from the carved symbols, were devoid of filth or signs of putrefaction. Where the pilgrims expected to hear buzzing, there was only the howl of the wind. Acting on a hunch, Armaan scanned the perimeter of the installation. About ten paces from the furthest corpse was a strip of earth darker than the surrounding ruins. It curved into the distance, and veered behind the pilgrims, forming a circle around the installation.

Armaan approached, lowered on one knee. At first, his mind did not register what he was seeing, but when he focused harder he realized the circle was formed of dead flies. Thousands of them, their bodies rigid and undamaged as though they had simply been struck dead within a few feet of the installation. Their wings glinted in the meager sunlight.

A chill of dread passed through Armaan's body. He stood up and approached his companions, head on a swivel. "Let's go. Now."

3

Within the downtown core, there were no roads to speak of, only loose pathways in and around the rubble. Survivors had established makeshift dwellings within the ruins, practically honeycombed one on top of the other. Only glimpses of them could be seen: the pale outline of a face, a toothless smile; the animalistic flash of fear-maddened eyes. The pilgrims did their best to ignore them as they moved closer to the movie palace.

Gone was the omnipresent dirge of the wind. In its place, the air rang with a chorus of screams and the occasional detonation of a makeshift bomb. The city had long become a battleground between various factions competing for resources and territory. Within the tent city, where the pilgrims called home, these conflicts were nothing more than hearsay, whispers. Now, the true scale and barbarism of these skirmishes were made plain to the outsiders. They were forced to use narrow tunnels and half-collapsed alleyways to circumvent the bloodshed. Combatants arrayed with makeshift armor—tire rubber, broken pieces of plywood, and metal siding—charged past the pilgrims, brandishing spears, bricks, machetes, and baseball bats studded with nails.

When they emerged from a particularly claustrophobic alley, the pilgrims encountered a second class of soldier. These were either completely nude—their bodies war-painted with ash—or clad in mail constructed with heavy scales of asphalt. Their breastplates were adorned with the cryptic emblem of the Carolith, spray-painted on or rubbed in with human waste. As the pilgrims scuttled across a collapsed bridge, one the nude fighters ran past them and into a crowd of waiting spearmen. The second he was impaled, the black device in his hand exploded, drowning the spearmen in a cloud of black smoke and a shower of blood.

Less than a block from the combat area, a building stood erroneously against a panorama of ruin. It was an imposing construction of red brick, with gargoyles perched on the corners of the roof. The marquis curved in a half circle around the face of the structure, the surviving letters suspended at odd angles, spelling nothing. A neon sign rose vertically from the center of the marquis. It was broken and the proprietors had tangled three flayed bodies through the lifeless glass tubing, as though to give the façade a touch of color, a sensational lure. Their mouths were frozen into horrified death screams. The pilgrims stopped and gaped at the structure, tears in their eyes.

At long last, their pilgrimage was complete.

THE TICKET BOOTH was blacked out with dust and dirt. Through the receiving window peered a face so altered by deformity it hardly looked like a face at all. Tumors sagged down the forehead and left cheek, obscuring one eye, while the other bulged from its socket, the white turned yellow by illness. The lips had been chewed away, leaving nothing but a layer of pinkish scar tissue. The gums were black and receded, the teeth abnormally long, thin, and exposed at the root. The nose was missing, the nasal cavity stuffed with a dirty rag.

"How many of you?" His visible eye darted over the pilgrims, but judging by his question he saw little or nothing. When the pilgrims were too stunned by shock and exhaustion to answer, he asked again, this time in a keening hiss, "How. Many. Of. You?"

Armaan took a tentative step forward. "Four," he said. Then quickly corrected himself, "Three. There are three of us."

The disfigured attendant shuffled around inside his booth. A moment later, a hand—callused, filth-encrusted but lacking deformity—emerged from the window holding three admission tickets. Armaan took them and handed one to Katy and Brian. The pilgrims stared in wonder at the pieces of cardboard. They were pristine, unbent, as though they had been printed that same day. Armaan raised the ticket to his nose and inhaled. The scent of fresh paper rushed directly to the pleasure centers of his brain. How long had been since he touched, smelled something new?

"Go inside. Show your tickets to the ticket taker," the attendant wheezed. "Don't just stand there. Tonight's an important night. Once the doors are closed, they're closed."

Armaan took Brian's hand, and Brian took Katy's hand, and together they entered the movie palace. The lobby was grand, baroque. A vaulted ceiling adorned with decorative plaster and copper filigree. A massive chandelier hung crooked from within a spiral of plasterwork, its prisms trailing clods of dust and ash so that it looked like the strung up carcass of something long dead—something that had been dragged from unimaginable oceanic depths.

Dozens of pilgrims, young and old, were scattered about the space, huddled against the walls, lying across the floor. Each bore some mark of their travels: scars, still-bleeding wounds, broken limbs, or the hint of a wasting disease; some stared in dumb wonder at their surroundings—tears glazing their eyes— while others slept or rocked back and forth, muttering to themselves. Despite the air of suffering, there was an almost tangible aura of anticipation crackling through the crowd—a collective bated breath.

Still hand-in-hand, the three pilgrims carefully picked their way through the supine bodies, searching for the ticket taker. As their gazes roved about the room, they noticed a banner strung

her cheeks.

Beside her, Brian cast his mind back to his childhood. He was playing in the park with his sister while their mother watched from a nearby bench. It was summer and both he and his sister were sweating from their game of tag. She was in close pursuit, hurling taunts and playful insults at his back, when she tripped over an exposed root and sprawled into the grass. Their mother stood and walked over, helping his sister to her feet, brushing the grass from her knees, the tears from her cheeks. It's okay, his mother said, you're okay. And she was. Brian recalled being so touched by his mother's cool-headed kindness, he approached and wrapped his arms around her. She smelled like the sun and clean laundry. In her embrace, he knew he was invulnerable to harm, that she could make all his pain and fear go away.

Armaan invoked a memory of when he attended university. It was Friday and he walked from his apartment to the house his best friend shared with two other roommates. They set up a foldout table and played beer pong until the sun was nearly extinguished and they were stumbling around, laughing from the alcohol. Later, more people arrived and the party grew so raucous the police were summoned. Seeing the red and blue lights reflected on the side of the house, Armaan grabbed the hand of the woman he'd been speaking to and made a mad dash for the baseball field behind the property. Once there, they bent over, hands on knees, and simultaneously laughed and gasped for air. The two of them—only having met that night—would become close friend throughout the duration of university.

Onscreen, the man on the bed screams. It's high and keening, more animal than human. Ski mask rolls him onto his back and plunges the blade into his stomach. The bed sheets transmute from slate grey to blackish red. The clip ends as ski mask pulls out a small handgun and shoots the man six times in the face. A close-up of the aftermath reveals a confusion of flesh and bone, a vague approximation of a mouth opening and closing like a beached fish. The camera pans again, catching a final glimpse of the window before slamming to black.

The pilgrims blinked like they had emerged from a dream. They exchanged tearful, smiling glances, feeling as though part of their humanity had been restored. Their memories were more alive than ever, encroaching on the black coagulation of fear polluting their minds. The audience around them was animated, cheering, blubbering, and moaning in what could have been terror or ecstasy. Drunk from nostalgia, Katy said, "I'm so happy we made the journey."

"Me too. Very much," Armaan said.

"I wish Brian were here."

They all nodded but said nothing, reluctant to disrupt their happiness.

Another title screen pulled their attention back toward the screen:

LAMENT #6 – THE INDEBTED.
FADE IN:
EXT. CITY STREET – NIGHT

A man in an expensive suit, his tie askew, expression harried, is being pushed down a sidewalk at gunpoint by two aggressors in masks, while—presumably—the cameraman walks backwards in front of the the businessman. You can hear him laughing, the proximity of his face behind the camera turning the sound into a low, tectonic rumble.

BUSINESMAN: Please. Oh God. I'll get you the—
GUNMAN #1: It's not back at the storage facility, you lying motherfucker.
BUSINESS: I don't…I don't know why it isn't there. Someone must've taken it.
GUNMAN #2: You're lucky we're in the open. Otherwise I'd shoot you in the back.
CUT TO:
INT HOUSE – NIGHT

The house is lavish but covered, floor to ceiling, with plastic sheeting. A chandelier glows like a dying star under a warped window of plastic. The gunman throws the businessman on the floor as the cameraman jerkily sets the camera on a tripod, ensuring everything is in frame.

The other aggressor fires his weapon twice, taking out each of the businessman's kneecaps. His screams are so loud, so frantic, the speakers crackle with distortion. He rolls around on the plastic sheeting as the man holsters his piece, picks up a crowbar and beats the businessman until his arms and chest bend out of shape.

As they watched, the pilgrims felt every blow in their teeth. They exchanged glances, confused. There was nothing for their memories to latch onto, only this sterile environment—splashes of red on white—and the all too familiar barrage of violence.

A few agonizing minutes later, the businessman is a bloody sprawl on the floor. One of the gunmen moves behind the camera and returns with a machete. With the assistance of his companion, he hacks at the businessman's neck—blood spurts, limbs twitch—until his head rolls away, jetting blood on the decapitator's shoes.

CUT TO...

An extreme close-up of the businessman's head: eyes wide and glazed, mouth hanging open, blood still trickling from his nostrils. Someone is holding it up as the camera operator walks backward, tracking the subject in slow motion. Eventually, they move outside and the camera pulls away from the disembodied head, revealing an expansive courtyard rimmed with cypress trees. The sun is a burnished medallion in a cradle of delicate clouds.

The pilgrims gasped.

The scene restored to Brian's mind the European trip he took with his now-deceased partner a year before the war. There had been a definite atmosphere of dread—every television in every coffee shop tuned to the news—but the couple still managed to enjoy their vacation. After all, it would likely be the last one they took in some time. War made recreational travel effectively impossible. And so, they spent most of their time outdoors—eschewing media exposure—visiting historic sites, hiking the countryside, dining on cobblestone patios.

On an exceptionally hot day, while sharing a bottle of ouzo,

Brian stared across the table at his partner. Her face was streaked with sweat, her hair wild from the humidity. And he wondered whether she would take him seriously if he asked her to marry him. They had once agreed that marriage wasn't for them, but the world was changing so drastically and violently, what had once seemed frivolous now carried a new significance. Marriage—an overt display of their love—could be a warding flare in this ever-darkening world. He continued to stare until she smiled affectionately, somewhat awkwardly, and asked what was wrong...

Everything below her neck abruptly disappeared, her throat turning red and ragged. The face lost its familiar shape, the eyes going dull, the skin blossoming into a garden of blood and bruises. Cringing in his seat, Brian squeezed the armrests, nauseous and gasping for air.

Onscreen, the man holding the head throws it out in front of him and kicks it like a football. It doesn't go very far—maybe a couple feet —before connecting with the courtyard and bouncing, the blood-soaked hair undulating with anemone grace.

As Brian's recollections merged unpleasantly with the film, Armaan managed to see beyond the cruelty onscreen as he sank into his own memories. The courtyard brought to mind the patio behind his grandmother's home. As a boy, he spent his summers there, using chalk to draw mythical creatures on the sun-warmed stones. He imagined the ornate flowerpots scattered around the area were home to beings made of twigs that protected his grandmother from harm. He wished now they were real, watching over his companions. But all they had were the Carolith, cruel, unfathomable, and made not of wood, but shadows and cold, hard stone.

Finally, Katy's disappointment from earlier sloughed away, replaced by a deep, near delirious, flood of happiness. She laughed silently, tears sliding down her cheeks. The sky...the sky in the film was so blue, so clear. She would give anything to stand under its immensity once again. It reminded her of after-school soccer games, family barbecues, and the scent of camp-fire...but those impressions mutated as the screen faded to black. Soccer games became a masked man kicking a severed head, family barbecues a group of starving, walking corpses cooking one of their own over a gasoline fire. And the smell: rich, heady, sickeningly sweet like spitted pork. Her hands trembled and she dropped the tin of popcorn.

A flurry of segments followed, pulling the pilgrims in and out of their memories like a slow drowning, every gasp for breath another precious scrap of something they had lost. Scenes of meticulous animal slaughter precipitated memories of long lost pets, their unfettered joy and innocence; a sequence featuring a school shooting from the head-mounted-camera perspective of the shooter prompted reminiscences of their high school years; and a graphic sex murder made them reflect on the opiate pleasure of intimacy, of reckless love.

However, these vignettes were scraped from their minds when a familiar landscape appeared onscreen—*a ruined gas station in a valley of rubble, its canopy leaning to one side, harboring shadows. The camera pans away from the ruins, focusing on a group of figures huddled in the distance. It approaches, its movements oddly smooth considering the uneven terrain. Closer now, the pilgrims come into view—four of them—sharing a single blanket under the gunmetal sky. And there is Geoff, alive, eye closed, blue lips moving in a dream.*

Brian, Katy, and Armaan inhaled sharply as a weight plunged into their bowels. The nostalgic high they had been riding—though gradually losing potency—finally dissipated, bleeding the color and optimism from their reanimated memories. They sank deeper into their seats and watched, silent and horrified, like prisoners hearing a verdict of death by execution.

The image onscreen jump cuts to a lower angle, the camera positioned on a flat surface. The pilgrims are framed in medium shot, and in the background stands what could only be one of the Carolith. Slender, impossibly tall, its body a single intricately carved and polished pillar of obsidian. No limbs or extremities are visible, no visage upon which to focus, though its gleaming surface seems to reflect—or emit from within—various shapes and hues, like colored water swirling in a glass bottle. The effect is both hypnotic and vaguely disturbing.

(Here the audience screamed, convulsed, cheered.)

In a series of stop motion cuts, the Carolith approaches the sleeping pilgrims. A blur of motion around its base as a shape—indistinct and spasmodically alive—twitches toward their wrinkling brows. Touching everyone but Geoff. The moment it makes contact, they startle awake. Another jump cut and the Carolith is gone, but the camera continues to roll as Brian, Katy, and Armaan rise with the sluggish, heavy locomotion of somnambulists.

Brian automatically reaches into his discarded coat and removes his utility knife. He extracts the blade as his companions watch, grips the handle in a white-knuckle grip, and hesitates. As though receiving silent off-screen instructions, he passes the knife to Armaan—Brian's former lover—who raises it above his head. He blinks and stabs Geoff in the neck.

Geoff's eyes snap open. Confusion transmutes to terror. He coughs once; blood gouts from his lips and splashes his chin. Armaan removes the blade and stabs him again, this time in the face. Steel penetrates flesh and glances off his cheekbone, gouging his left eye. The orb bursts, gushing vitreous humor like a spontaneous flood of tears. He screams and Armaan responds by stabbing him a third time, in the chest. Brian and Katy descend upon him with fingers and teeth, widening his new orifices to reach the meat, the marrow. Geoff thrashes, squeals, and cries for his mother. The camera pulls in as Katy tears away the first hunk of flesh from his neck, chewing and swallowing with a kind of detached ecstasy. Her pupils are fully dilated and in their darkness shapes and colors churn, flicker.

Watching the screen, Katy touched her lips. Her tongue still carried the taste of Geoff's blood. The sensation was more vivid, more real, than any memory she had revisited that night. She knew then their quest to reclaim what they had lost had been in vain.

5

The pilgrims watched the remainder of the film in a fugue state. On the periphery of their awareness—like sounds heard outside a nightmare—a series of victims screamed and begged for their lives, flesh burst open with wet rending sounds, blood bubbled

PREVIOUS
APPEARANCES

"Walking in Ash" *Pluto in Furs*, Ed. Scott Dwyer
"Mother's Mark" *Forbidden Futures #7*, Ed. Cody Goodfellow
"Apate's Children" *Teenage Grave*, Ed. Ira Rat
"The Human Clay" *The New Flesh: A Literary Tribute to David Cronenberg*, Eds. Sam Richard & Brendan Vidito
"The Chimera Session" *Ripe*, Eds. Eleanore Studer and Manuel Chavarria
"Church of the Chronically Ill" *The Other Stories Podcast*
"The Living Column" *Pluto in Furs 2*, Ed. Scott Dwyer
"Nostalgia Night at the Snuff Palace" *Cinema Viscera*, Ed. Sam Richard

ABOUT THE AUTHOR

Brendan Vidito is the author of the Wonderland Award-winning collection of body horror stories, *Nightmares in Ecstasy* (Clash Books, 2018). He also co-edited the Splatterpunk-Award-nominated anthology *The New Flesh: A Literary Tribute to David Cronenberg* (Weirdpunk Books, 2019) with Sam Richard. He lives in Ontario, surrounded by books and reptiles.

ALSO FROM WEIRDPUNK BOOKS

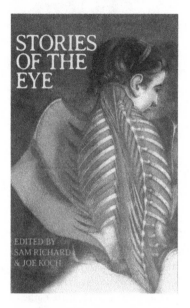

Stories of the Eye edited by Sam Richard & Joe Koch

An anthology of horror stories exploring the relationships between artists and their subjects. Featuring stories from Andrew Wilmot, M. Lopes da Silva, Gwendolyn Kiste, Hailey Piper, Roland Blackburn, Ira Rat, Donyae Coles, Matt Neil Hill, Brendan Vidito, LC von Hessen, Gary J. Shipley, and editors Joe Koch and Sam Richard. *Stories of the Eye* violently explores the connection of art to the body, the cosmos, madness, depression, grief, trauma, and so much more.s

To Wallow in Ash & Other Sorrows by Sam Richard

Winner of the 2019 Wonderland Award for Best Collection, *To Wallow in Ash & Other Sorrows* is a bleak and unflinching look at widowhood through the lens of horror fiction. Written in the early days of widowhood and in the spirit of J.G. Ballard, Kathe Koja, and Georges Bataille, these stories are a cross-section of literary splatterpunk, transgressive fiction, and weird horror, which explore loss, grief, and the alluring comforts found within the heart of oblivion. This Revised & Expanded version includes the never-before-seen novelette *There is Power in the Blood*.

"With *To Wallow in Ash & Other Sorrows*, Sam Richard has crafted a book of stories that will rip your heart right out of your chest... and it's absolutely worth every moment."

— GWENDOLYN KISTE, AUTHOR OF *THE RUST MAIDENS* AND *THE INVENTION OF GHOSTS*

Cinema Viscera: An Anthology of Movie Theater Horror edited by Sam Richard

In five unique and bizarre tales Katy Michelle Quinn (*Girl in the Walls*), Charles Austin Muir (*Slippery When Metastasized*), Jo Quenell (*The Mud Ballad*), Brendan Vidito (*Nightmares in Ecstasy*), and Sam Richard (*Sabbath of the Fox-Devils*) each bring you their own disturbing vision of what lurks in the darkness of your local movie theater.

Not gonna lie, this shit is a lot darker than we thought it would be.

Make sure to grab some popcorn...

WEIRDPUNK
STATEMENT

Thank you for picking up this Weirdpunk book!
We're a small press out of Minneapolis, MN and our goal is to publish interesting and unique titles in all varieties of weird horror and splatterpunk. It is our hope that if you like one of our releases, you will like the others.
If you enjoyed this book, please check out what else we have to offer, drop a review, and tell your friends about us.
Buying directly from us is the best way to support what we do.
www.weirdpunkbooks.com

Printed in the USA
CPSIA information can be obtained
at www.ICGtesting.com
LVHW040908190923
758435LV00006B/472

9 781951 658236